# Wiggie Wins the West

Books by Elisabet McHugh

*Beethoven's Cat*
*Wiggie Wins the West*

# WIGGIE
# WINS THE WEST

*by Elisabet McHugh*
*illustrated by Anita Riggio*

ATHENEUM   1989   NEW YORK

Text copyright © 1989 by Elisabet McHugh
Illustrations copyright © 1989 by Anita Riggio

Atheneum
Macmillan Publishing Company
866 Third Avenue, New York, NY 10022
Collier Macmillan Canada, Inc.
First Edition   Printed in the United States of America
10  9  8  7  6  5  4  3  2  1

Library of Congress Cataloging-in-Publication Data
McHugh, Elisabet.
Wiggie wins the west/by Elisabet McHugh;
illustrated by Anita Riggio.—1st ed.   p.   cm.
Summary: A long car trip through the West provides the
boastful cat Wiggie with many opportunities to save the
human and animal members of his family, who sometimes
do not realize how brave, selfless, and brilliant he is.
ISBN 0-689-31449-3
[1. Cats—Fiction.   2. West (U.S.)—Fiction.]
I. Riggio, Anita, ill.   II. Title.
PZ7.M47863Wi   1989   [Fic]—dc19   88-8176   CIP   AC

*This book is
for Karen
—E.M.*


*For Katie, John Fitz,
Joseph, and Frank,
with love
—A.R.*

# Wiggie Wins the West

# ONE

That fateful morning when it all began, Josh and I were upstairs in Cilla's room. We were trying out the bunk beds she had bought for us recently at a garage sale. It was actually a large doll's bed, but the size was perfect even for my unusually well-proportioned figure. I was now occupying the top bunk while Josh was curled up on the bottom one. The bed was standing on top of Cilla's dresser.

I was rearranging my blanket when Winston, the family bulldog, came barging into the room.

1

"Hey, guys," he rasped, slightly out of breath, "guess what?"

Interrupting my task, I turned around and glanced at the familiar potbellied figure.

"You'll never believe what I just heard," he continued.

Refusing to be drawn into any kind of conversation, I stifled a yawn while continuing to paw at my blanket.

"I almost didn't believe it myself." Winston looked at us with his big, watery eyes. For some reason they were bulging more than usual.

It was evident that he was expecting some kind of response. "Don't tell me," I said. "You found the bone you've been looking for since last spring."

"Bone?" His face was blank. "Who said anything about a bone? This is something that concerns the family. All of us."

Now Josh finally stirred. He peeked over the edge of his bed. "You mean we're going on another picnic?"

Since we had been on a picnic the previous afternoon, that didn't seem very likely.

"Nope." Winston plumped down in the middle of the floor, which as usual was littered with a varied assortment of Cilla's belongings. "It's Mr. Carter.

2

He's leaving tomorrow morning for another job interview."

Was that all? Since Mr. C. received his Ph.D. back in May, he had already been interviewed by three colleges in two different states. He was also considering a position right here in town.

I suppressed another yawn. "Let me see," I said in a bored voice. "This will be his fourth trip, right?"

Josh, who had already lost interest, closed his eyes.

"He'll be gone four days this time." Winston licked his chops. For some reason he seemed unable to settle down. He kept changing position and his ears were twitching. "And guess where he's going? You won't believe me when I tell you."

"And why not?" I asked, a trifle impatiently. I wondered why he insisted on making such a big deal over nothing. Digging myself a little deeper into my fuzzy blue blanket, I added, "Unless, of course"—here I chuckled to show my keen sense of humor—"he's going to China."

Winston fastened his protruding eyes on me. "Not exactly," he said. "But he's going to Moscow."

Closing my eyes, I murmured tiredly, "Well, I hope he has a nice—*what did you say?*" I sat bolt upright.

4

"I said he's going to Moscow."

I eyed him suspiciously. "Are you by any chance referring to the capital of Russia?"

"Is there another one?"

"Ha, ha." Josh guffawed suddenly. "Tried to fool us, didn't you? You're just kidding, right?"

"No, I'm not," Winston said earnestly. "I swear. Mr. C. is really going to Moscow."

"What on earth for?"

"I just told you. For an interview."

"All the way to Russia?" I said skeptically. "I can understand why he would go to West Virginia, and South Carolina, but *Russia* . . . ?"

"I'm only telling you what I heard." Winston sounded annoyed. "Maybe he's going because the pay is good. Or maybe the weather there is nice."

By now all thought of sleep had been banished from my mind, and my brain was working overtime. The more I thought about this unexpected piece of news, the more sinister it seemed. Russia? Why would Mr. C. even consider moving halfway around the world? And what about the rest of the family? What did Mrs. C. think about this?

My own noble ancestors had, of course, lived on the other side of the Atlantic, but personally I preferred to remain in the good old U. S. of A. And if for some reason I really *had* to move to a foreign country, Russia was sure to be at the bottom of my list.

"Anyway," Winston added, "Mr. C. may not get the job or even want it after he gets there. We are probably worrying about nothing."

I slumped back on my bed. Winston was right, of course.

"On the other hand"—he scratched his belly noisily—"who knows, he just *may* decide to accept it. . . ."

Trying to ignore the fluttery feeling in my stomach, I said, in a feeble attempt at lightheartedness, "Well, in that case we'd better brace ourselves. One wrong step and we could all end up in a labor camp in Siberia. . . ."

Now Josh came to life. "You mean they might think Mr. C. is a spy?"

"Of course." I peeked down at him from my top bunk. "They think all Americans are spies."

Winston licked his chops. "The possibility has already occurred to me," he admitted. "Suspicious bunch, that's what they are."

I didn't know that Gwendolyn, the neighbor's white Persian cat, had joined us until she suddenly spoke up.

"They all look like turnips," she said.

We stared blankly at her.

"Or beets, maybe. Giant beets."

I wondered what she was talking about. But, since Gwendolyn—even in her best moments—is hardly the brightest specimen, it was quite possible she didn't know what she was talking about herself.

"Beets?" I said uncertainly. "You mean the Russians look like beets?" I had never met any of them in person, but the Russian premier was frequently on television. As far as I could remember, in no way did he resemble a beet. Or, for that matter, a turnip.

"The buildings, of course." Gwenny's voice held a slight note of reproof. "Don't you remember the movie we saw, Wiggie? *The Invasion of the Russian Werewolves?* The buildings in Moscow have roofs that look like upside-down turnips. Or beets."

Light dawned on me. I let out a sigh of relief. For a moment I had thought that her brain had somehow finally dissolved.

"Eh . . . you're so right. They do look like turnips. Or," I added hastily, "beets."

"Upside down."

"Upside down."

There was a moment's silence. Then Winston said, "The Russians will probably plant bugs in our apartment."

"Probably." Josh looked depressed at the thought. "All over the place."

"Even the bathroom."

Gwenny said timidly, "I don't think you have to worry about bugs."

"No?" I raised my eyebrows. "And why not?"

"Because," she explained, "I'm sure the Carters will bring plenty of bug spray."

Josh started snickering, and Winston was overcome by a sudden cough attack.

I took a deep breath while slowly counting to five. "It's not *that* kind of bugs," I said patiently. "We're talking about sophisticated listening devices. Tape recorders. Hidden microphones."

Gwenny looked at me with her mouth open. I could tell that her minuscule brain was trying very hard to assimilate the information.

"All the houses in Russia probably have microphones already built in," Josh commented.

Winston scratched his chest. "Standard equipment," he agreed gloomily. "For them, that is."

Gradually Gwendolyn's face lost its vacant look. "You mean when you move into an apartment the bugs are already installed?" she asked.

I nodded.

"Just like a dishwasher?"

Now it was Winston's turn to snicker.

"Er . . . yes . . . kind of." I didn't feel up to trying to explain things to her again. "Something like that."

"Or a kitchen range?"

"Ah . . . well . . . I guess so."

"And you don't have to pay extra for it?"

Now Winston was laughing hysterically, while Josh and I were staring at Gwenny in openmouthed fascination.

"Uh . . . no," I said at last. "It's paid for by the . . . er . . ." I scratched my head. ". . . by the . . ."

". . . by the government," Josh filled in.

"Really?" Gwendolyn sounded pleased. "I think that's wonderful."

I couldn't believe my ears. *"Wonderful?"* I exclaimed agitatedly. "You think a place with microphones built into the walls is *wonderful?"*

"Why, of course." She seemed surprised. "Imagine a built-in convenience that we don't have here. I bet the Carters will love Moscow."

# TWO

Later that afternoon I was stretched out under the apple tree in the Carters' backyard. A soft breeze moving gently through the leaves tickled my tummy, which at the moment was causing me some discomfort.

Mrs. C. had decided to clean out the refrigerator and, never one to shirk honest work, I had volunteered my services. Now the combination of dried-up sardines, cheddar cheese, moldy baloney, condensed milk, and a funny-smelling slice of meat loaf made me feel rather queasy.

The news of Mr. C.'s upcoming trip to Moscow had completely ruined my morning nap. I was now attempting to get some much-needed rest while Stevie, the ten-year-old member of the family, was gone. In the ensuing peace and tranquility, I felt my eyelids grow increasingly heavy. At the same time, my sensitive nose picked up the first indication of tonight's dinner—the tangy aroma of barbecued chicken.

Mr. C., who was in charge of tonight's cookout, was just about to place a plump, juicy sausage on the grill. This was the treat he always reserved for himself while doing the cooking. Exhausted as I was, I decided not to try for any handouts until later. I was slowly drifting off to sleep when a voice unexpectedly broke the silence.

"Wiggie?"

Carefully, I opened one eye. Just as I had feared. There was Gwendolyn again.

"Wiggie?" she repeated.

Not feeling very sociable, I closed my eye, limiting myself to a simple "uhum."

"Are you sleeping?"

"Uhum."

"I see." Her voice was apologetic. "Well, I'll talk to you when you wake up."

"Talk to me about what?"

"About my move."

"What move?"

"My move over here. To live with you."

I sat up with a jerk. My stomach made a loud, gurgling sound. Staring wildly at her, I croaked, "Live with *us*?"

"You mean you didn't know?"

Still unnerved by the shock, I stammered, "Why on earth would you come to live with us?"

Gwenny rubbed her nose with her paw. "Kathy's grandmother had another heart attack last month, and she is now moving in with the Bowers. Unfortunately, the grandmother is allergic to cats, so Kathy was told she'd have to find another home for me. Last night when Cilla heard about it, she asked her parents if I could come and live with you."

I swallowed. "And they said you could?"

Gwenny nodded. "They thought it was a great idea, since we all get along so well and everything."

I experienced a sinking feeling in my stomach. Gwendolyn really was going to move in with us. Not that I had anything against her, of course. She was a kindhearted soul, and she and I had been friends for years. The problem was that her brain was about the size of a very small split pea. Any prolonged conversation with her tended to drive me to the brink of a nervous breakdown. My visits next

12

door were usually short-lived, and I was always relieved to get back home to my own pals.

Reminding myself now of the possibility that the Carters might be moving to Russia, I wondered whether Gwenny had any idea what she was getting into.

"I know I'm going to be just as happy here," she continued. "This has always been my dream, you know."

I stared dumbly at her. "It has?"

"I've always wanted to be able to spend more time with you, Wiggie."

Well, *that* I could understand.

"In a way, you have always been my idol. Someone that I could look up to and admire."

I realized now that Gwenny probably was brighter than she looked. Maybe I had been a little too hard on her in the past. It could be that the privilege of associating with me had somehow increased the capacity of her brain cells.

"You always seem to know so much about everything." Gazing wistfully at me with her liquid blue eyes, she added, "I wish I were as smart as you."

Clearing my throat, I replied modestly, "Well, not everyone can be a genius, you know. I just happen to be one of the lucky ones, that's all."

Despite my superior IQ and my noble heritage

(my ancestors were intimately associated with the royal courts in Europe), I have always tried to maintain a low profile. Naturally, this hasn't always been easy.

Gwenny sighed deeply. "I just can't wait until next week," she said.

"Next week?"

"That's when I'm moving in with you. A week from today."

"Oh, that." I hadn't known it was going to happen so soon.

Actually, once I got used to the idea, it didn't seem all that bad. It would, in fact, be downright cruel to deprive this poor girl of my intellectual and cultural companionship. I could picture her curled up at my feet, listening breathlessly to the profound words of wisdom falling from my lips.

I wondered how my pals would take it. Neither Josh, the black-and-white feline who happens to be my closest friend, nor Winston were home at the moment.

Noticing that my stomach finally had settled down, I once more became aware of the tempting smells coming from the barbecue. Deciding that the time had come to replenish my energy with a juicy piece of grilled chicken, I headed for the patio.

"Well," Gwenny said as she followed me across the lawn, "what do you think about it?"

"About what?" Already my mind was occupied by the upcoming delights.

"About me coming to live with you?"

"Oh, that." I kept forgetting.

"I hope Josh and Winston won't mind."

"Of course they won't."

"Are you sure?"

"Don't worry. I'll talk to them."

"I don't know how I'd ever manage without you, Wiggie." Gwenny gazed admiringly at me. "You're always so sure of yourself."

"I know." It was hard to keep my superior intelligence from shining through. "Just another sign of my leadership qualities, I guess."

We had reached the patio. When Mr. C. spotted us he took a piece of chicken from the grill and removed the skin. Now he dropped this golden tidbit in front of me. I was just about to dig in when I became aware of Gwenny. She was sitting timidly behind me.

Conscious of the fact that the responsibility for this poor girl now rested entirely with me, I heroically pushed the chicken skin over to her. "Here," I said, "be my guest."

"Oh, Wiggie," Gwenny breathed. "You're so good to me."

The crunching sound as she devoured this delectable snack made me wish I hadn't been quite so good.

"Quite the gentleman today, aren't you, Wiggie?" Mr. C. said now. "Well, here's for you."

A large chunk of juicy chicken meat suddenly appeared in front of my nose.

Wow! Without wasting any time I grabbed it, carrying it off to the side of the patio. Even my pal Josh might challenge me over such a feast. Keeping a paw on the meat, I looked around. Fortunately, he still was nowhere to be seen.

As I chomped away on my delicious snack, I decided that this was definitely my best day so far this week. Maybe Gwenny would continue to bring me good luck. The day wasn't over yet, either. I still had dinner to look forward to—first my own and then the family's. Not to mention my share of the potato chips that Stevie always munches on while reading comics in bed. And the chocolate chip cookies that his older sister, Cilla, is addicted to. And the tuna sandwiches that Mr. C. usually makes while watching the late movies. And . . .

# THREE

"Obviously, something has to be done." I looked down at the others from my elevated position on the kitchen counter.

"Yep," Josh agreed.

Winston nodded.

"Gwenny?"

She looked up at me. "If you think so, Wiggie."

"I do. We have to make a plan."

"Yep," Josh said again.

Winston grunted in assent.

"Mr. C. left for Moscow two days ago," I continued. "There is a distinct possibility that he might decide to take the job there."

"Yep."

"We can't allow that to happen."

"Nope."

Winston rubbed his ear. "I'm with you," he said, "but I really don't see what we can do about it."

Neither did I, but this wasn't the time to admit that.

"Let's pool our ideas," I suggested.

"Yep."

I glared irritably at Josh. "And will you quit saying 'yep' all the time? Is that the only word you know?"

"Yep . . . I mean, sure thing, Wiggie."

"Instead of watching Westerns every night," I commented rather acidly, "maybe you should go to bed."

"But I do go to bed," Josh protested, "as soon as the last show is over and Mr. C. turns off the TV."

I decided to ignore him. Lately, he had been a real pain in the neck.

"We don't want to live in a place where at any time we might get arrested and tortured," I began again. "As citizens of the greatest country in the world, namely the United States of America, we have the right to enjoy the freedom and liberty that our forefathers secured for us. It's unreasonable to expect us to move to a country like Russia, which is chock full of spies, KGB agents, and secret police. A country . . ."

"I thought they didn't do that anymore," Josh said suddenly.

"Didn't do what?"

"Arrest people. And torture them."

I sighed exasperatedly. "Says who?"

"I don't remember." Josh scratched his ear. "There's been a lot about it on television."

"Well," I snapped, "I've watched lots of movies on television, too, and believe me, Russia is crawling with spies and KGB agents." I had especially enjoyed the movie with James Bond, the name of which I couldn't recall at the moment.

". . . a country where there is a sad lack of human rights, and probably"—here I chuckled to show that I was able to joke even in the face of disaster—"an even sadder lack of animal rights. A country where a knock on the door in the middle of the night means that you will be taken away, never to be heard from again. A country . . ."

I was gradually becoming aware of the fact that someone was poking me in the back, trying to get my attention. Turning, I discovered that Gwenny had jumped up behind me on the counter. "Wiggie," she whispered timidly, "there is something I think you should know. . . ."

I frowned at being interrupted again, just as I was warming up to my subject. "Later," I said impatiently.

". . . a country," I repeated, looking solemnly down at my audience, "where nothing is sacred. A country that treats its citizens . . ."

"But, Wiggie . . ." Gwenny kept tugging at my coat.

"*Please,* Gwen," I hissed. "Not *now.* . . ."

Raising my voice, I picked up where I had left off. ". . . a country that treats its citizens in the most despicable manner. A country that accuses all foreigners of spying and that . . ."

I continued in the same vein for another four or five minutes, sharing my vast reservoirs of knowledge with the others. Josh kept yawning and nodding off, a sure proof of the consequences of late-night television watching. Winston was stretched out on the floor, his head resting on his paws. His eyes were closed, but I could tell from his twitching ears that I had his full attention.

Gwendolyn had left the room, which didn't surprise me since most of what I had been saying was beyond the scope of her limited intelligence, anyway.

". . . and so," I finished with a flourish, "it's up to

20

us to save the family. The security and welfare of everyone in this household is resting squarely on our shoulders."

I paused for a moment. "Any suggestions?"

There was no response.

Josh was leaning against the sink cabinet. His chin was resting on his chest, and for a moment I thought he was studying something on the floor. Then, suddenly, an unmistakable snore was heard.

"Josh!" I said sharply.

Another snore.

Annoyed, I turned my attention to Winston. "Well, old pal," I said, "what do you think we should do?"

Winston's ear twitched, but his eyes were still closed.

"Don't you think," I said, "that, based on my observations, we could . . ."

Winston moved his head and mumbled groggily, "Is it morning already?" Then he blinked a couple of times before focusing his bulging eyes on me. "Oh," he said, "it's you. I just had the weirdest dream. There was this big, fat . . ."

"You were sleeping," I said accusingly.

"Sleeping?" Winston scratched his ear. "Well, I . . . now that you . . ." He interrupted himself and looked over at Josh, who was still snoring. "Of

course I wasn't sleeping," he said unconvincingly.
"What made you think that?"

"Did you listen to what I was saying?"

Now Winston looked affronted. "Of course I did.
Every single word."

"And how did you like my speech?"

"Like it? Oh . . . it was . . . uh . . . great. Simply
. . . uh . . ." He scratched his belly noisily. "Simply
. . . er . . . inspiring."

"I know," I said modestly. "Sometimes I think I
should go into politics."

I dwelt on this pleasant prospect for a moment
before returning to more imminent matters. "So," I
said briskly, "what should we do?"

Winston looked puzzled. "Do about what?"

"How can we stop Mr. C. from dragging us away
to Russia?"

"Oh, that." He cleared his throat. "Eh . . . maybe
we should wait until he gets back from Moscow. He
probably doesn't like it there, anyway."

"But he does." That was Gwendolyn speaking.

Startled by her sudden reappearance, I said irritably, "I wish you wouldn't sneak up on people like
that."

Winston licked his chops. "What was that you
said again, Gwenny?"

"Mr. C. loves Moscow."

"Uh . . . really?"

"How do you know?" I asked.

"Mrs. C. just talked to him on the phone. He took the job."

Both Winston and I stared dumbly at her.

"He . . . he *did*?" I croaked finally.

"That's what I was trying to tell you earlier." She looked reproachfully at me. "Now Mr. C. has to find a house for us to live in. He won't be back until Sunday."

"Gee . . ." Winston swallowed nervously. "I never *really* thought . . ."

"Mrs. C. also told him that she is going to talk to Kathy and her parents. She wants to make sure it's all right for me to move with you to Moscow. Especially since you are going to stay there for almost a whole year."

"Russia," I said dully. I still couldn't believe it. "We're moving to Moscow, Russia."

"No, we're not," Gwenny said.

"Huh?"

Calmly, she repeated, "We're not moving to Moscow, Russia."

"We're not?"

"But you just said we were." Winston looked confused.

"No, I didn't."

"You said that Mr. C. took the job in Moscow, and now he's looking for a house and won't come home until Sunday."

"That's right." Gwenny coughed delicately. "However, there seems to be a slight mix-up regarding the place he is visiting. Mr. C. is not in Moscow, Russia." She paused. "He's in Moscow, Idaho."

# FOUR

"*Moscow, Idaho?*"

"*Moscow, Idaho?*" Josh echoed.

Winston sat up. "Idaho, huh?" He reached under his arm to scratch himself.

"That's in the United States," Gwenny informed us.

"I know," I said, a trifle impatiently.

"Out West somewhere."

I frowned. "I know that, too." Actually, I had been thinking of Idaho as being next to Florida, but then it's easy to get things mixed up when your brain is as crammed with geographical facts as mine is.

"The West, huh?" Winston transferred the scratching to his left hindquarters. It made a grating sound. I wondered if he had fleas.

Josh looked thoughtful. "The wide, open spaces of the West," he murmured. "Where the buffalo roam."

"I thought buffalo roamed the prairie."

"Wild mustangs . . . and cowboys," Josh continued.

"What about Indians?" Gwenny asked timidly.

"I was just going to mention them," Josh said. "Lots of saloons in the West, too. And gunfights."

"Kathy's dad used to watch those all the time."

"Watch what?"

"The gunfights. On television."

Although I was listening with half an ear, I took no part in the conversation. Something was stirring in the back of my mind. Some kind of information that had to do with the West. I rubbed my nose, trying to remember. It concerned the family, that much I knew.

Suddenly it came to me.

"Mr. C.'s great-grandfather lived out West," I said. They all looked at me.

"He took his family and left New York. They went out West to settle."

After a moment's silence, Winston said, "Where did you hear that?"

"Mr. C. was telling Cilla about it a couple of years ago. She had a school assignment where she was supposed to find out which country her family originally came from and where and when they settled over here."

"And Mr. C.'s great-grandfather came from New York?"

I eyed Josh coolly. "Of course not. He and his wife came from Germany. They got off the ship in New York and stayed there until their first child was born. Then they left for . . . uh . . . Wyoming, I think, because they wanted to have some land of their own." I frowned, trying to remember what else Mr. C. had said. "A few years later the town where they lived needed a marshal. Nobody else wanted the job, so he took that on, too. But he still worked his ranch."

"No kidding." Winston was finally done scratching himself. "I suppose they crossed the country in a covered wagon, huh?"

"Probably."

"You mean like the people in 'Little House on the

28

Prairie'?" Gwendolyn sighed dreamily. "How romantic."

I said dryly, "Believe me, crossing the plains in those days was not exactly a picnic. Lots of people were killed by the Indians."

"And scalped," Josh added.

Gwenny turned pale. "Do they still do that?"

"Do what?"

She swallowed. "Scalp people."

"I don't think so." Winston sounded uncertain.

Josh guffawed. "Of course they don't," he said. He turned to me. "Do they, Wiggie?"

I pretended to be busy licking my paw. Did the Indians still scalp people? A cold shiver went up my spine. For all I knew they were still at it.

This was followed by an alarming thought. Was Moscow, Idaho, going to be even more dangerous than Moscow, Russia?

"Wiggie?"

"Eh . . . certain tribes," I said cautiously, "may still be keeping up the practice. However"—I shrugged to show that personally I wasn't really worried—"most Indians nowadays are peaceful."

Everyone looked relieved.

I could tell that now something else was on Gwenny's mind. Her face had an expression of fierce concentration, indicating that her brain was working overtime.

"Wiggie," she asked finally, "did you say that Mr. C.'s great-grandfather came over from Germany?"

I nodded. "With his wife. I believe they had been married only about a year when they decided to leave the Old Country."

She looked puzzled. "What Old Country?"

"Germany, of course. I just told you."

"I didn't know Germany was that old."

Slowly, I counted to ten. "It's just an expression," I explained patiently. "Whatever European country you came from, that was the Old Country. The United States is the New Country."

"Oh." Gwenny stared blankly at me. Her mouth was open. I shook my head and sighed. God only knew, I had done my best to educate her.

"Is there anything else you want to know?" I asked now.

"Well," she said apologetically, "I was just wondering if they brought their cat."

"Cat?" What was she talking about now? "What cat?"

"Did Mr. C.'s great-grandfather and his wife bring their cat over from Germany?"

I scratched my head. As far as I could remember, Mr. C. had made no reference whatsoever to cats. I was just going to tell Gwenny this when she continued.

"I only wondered if it was on this occasion that your great-great-whatever-grandfather came over, Wiggie."

It took me a few seconds to catch the implication of her remark. As the idea gradually sank in, I felt a shiver of excitement. Could it be possible? Was this the explanation for my family's presence on this side of the Atlantic? From the royal courts of Europe (where my most-famous ancestor, Ludwig I, had spent his life) to the majestic mountains and open plains of the American West . . . ? Yes, I told myself a moment later, this was the way it must have happened.

"Wiggie? Are you all right?" Gwenny sounded worried.

Clearing my throat, I said, "It's funny that you should mention it, Gwenny." I gazed solemnly at her. "This young couple did, indeed, bring with them not only one cat, but two. And as you have already figured out, those were my great-great-whatever-grandparents." Overcome with emotion at the thought of this newly discovered link with my past, I swallowed and dabbed my eyes with my paw.

"How come you never told us any of this before?" Winston asked suspiciously.

31

"Yeah," Josh echoed. "How come?"

"Well." I made a deprecating gesture. "I really didn't think you'd be interested. You already knew I had my roots in Europe. It's obvious that someone in my family emigrated to this country, or I wouldn't be here today."

I paused, thinking of the courage it must have taken to leave everything behind and venture into the unknown. . . . But then, of course, those two felines were probably just like me—bold, adventurous, filled with true pioneer spirit, ready to endure whatever hardships that lay ahead in order to . . .

"So Mr. C.'s great-grandfather was a marshal, huh?" Winston's bulging eyes focused on me. "Must have been a pretty dangerous job in those days."

"Well," I commented, "I'm sure it still is."

"What do you mean?"

I shrugged. "It's quite obvious, really. Just because we happen to live in a civilized state like Virginia, that doesn't mean that the rest of the country is equally civilized. On the contrary, a number of states—particularly those out West—have probably changed very little since the days when Mr. C.'s great-grandfather and my ancestors crossed the plains."

I let this information sink in for a moment. "We all watch the news on television from time to time, right? Well, did you ever hear anyone mention Wyoming? Or, for that matter, Idaho?" I looked around at my pals.

"Of course not," I continued. "And do you know why? Because they haven't caught up with the twentieth century yet. They may have cars and passable roads nowadays, but probably very little else. If they had big, modern cities, then we'd be sure to hear about the big-city crime rate. But who, in this day and age, wants to hear about a saloon shootout? Or a buffalo stampede? Or an Indian attack?"

I shook my head. "Believe me, the West is as rugged and lawless today as it was a hundred years ago."

I was already convinced that my own ancestors had assisted the marshal in upholding law and order. They might on occasion even have saved his life.

What could be more fitting than having me, their direct descendant, assume the same kind of responsibility during our journey westward? Obviously, it would take someone with my fearless character and rugged personality to protect Mr. C. and his family, and to see them safely to their destination.

I looked around at my pals. How pampered and spoiled they were! How carefree their existence! I sighed. I hoped they realized how lucky they were to have me to look after them. The journey ahead would no doubt be filled with dangers and hardships that would strain my capabilities to the limit. Yet, I knew that regardless of what might happen, I would never give up, never leave their side.

For a moment the thought of my own unselfish personality and my willingness to put my life on the line choked me up.

Again I sighed as I looked at the others. How innocent and trusting they were! Well, I decided, they might as well stay that way. I knew now that the heavy burden of my mission would not be lifted until both they and the rest of the family were securely settled in their log cabin in the primitive frontier town of Moscow, Idaho.

# FIVE

During the next few weeks life was rather hectic as the whole family was getting ready for the move. Even Cilla was so busy that she hardly had any time for me.

The morning before our departure Winston was still asleep on the back porch after a late night out. Gwendolyn had gone over to the Bowers, and Josh and I were in the kitchen.

B. C., who recently had celebrated his first birthday, was sitting in his high chair. After successfully dumping his bowl of cereal on the floor, he was now busy hitting the table with his spoon. Mrs. C. had vanished upstairs and could be heard arguing with Stevie, while sounds from outside indicated that Mr. C. was still struggling to fit everyone's belongings into the back of the pickup truck.

I did my best to ignore the commotion. The hollow feeling in my stomach brought to mind the more urgent matter of breakfast. I looked with satisfaction at my food bowl. This morning it was filled to the brim with Feline Feast's moist salmon-flavored nuggets, a brand the Carters had switched to recently. As far as taste went it was a definite improvement over my usual dry Meow-Chow.

As soon as my worst hunger was appeased, I said to Josh, "I wonder what Winston is up to nowadays. He sure doesn't spend much time at home."

At first I didn't think Josh was listening, but then, rather absentmindedly, he looked up from his food. "Uh . . . did you say something, Wiggie?"

"I just said that Winston seems to be gone a lot."

Josh's only reaction was to stare blankly at me, a sure indication that he had other things on his mind. After a moment he said vaguely, "How about that?" before lapsing into silence again.

I looked sharply at him. Lately he had been behaving rather strangely.

"What's the matter, old pal?" I asked. "Did you have a fight with . . . eh . . . what's-her-name?"

Since Josh changed girlfriends all the time, I frequently got their names mixed up. I was pretty sure his current flame was Daisy, but then again she might already have been replaced by someone else.

Now, at least, I had Josh's attention. "Honeypot and I never fight," he informed me.

*"Honeypot?"*

"Eh . . . that's what I call her." He looked slightly flustered. "Her real name is Hermoine Patou. She's French."

"No kidding? What happened to Daisy?"

"Who?"

"Daisy. Don't tell me you've forgotten her already."

"Of course not." It was obvious that he had. "We were just friends. Honeypot is the girl I've been looking for all my life."

I sighed, wondering how many times I'd heard him say that. "I hope you haven't forgotten that we're moving tomorrow."

With a self-satisfied air, Josh started cleaning his whiskers. "Of course not. But Honeypot is going to wait for me."

*"Wait* for you? But we'll be gone for a whole year."

"So what?" His eyes were dreamy. "In a relationship like ours, time is of no importance. True love will survive anything."

I was just going to remind him that none of his former true loves had survived more than a month when Stevie came bursting into the kitchen. I just barely avoided being trampled to a pulp by retreating underneath the table. Following behind him was Mrs. C.

True to pattern, Stevie headed straight for the refrigerator. When he emerged again he had a loaf of French bread in one hand and a jar of peanut butter in the other. His mouth was filled with jelly doughnut. "It's not fair," he complained between swallows, "that Cilla gets to bring her TV when I don't."

Mrs. C. replied tiredly, "It so happens that she has a TV that works."

"So do I."

"Really? Since when?"

"The sound works. It just doesn't have any picture."

"Well, you can't bring it and that's it." Mrs. C. began to clean up the mess on the floor. "Why don't you go outside and help your father?"

To my relief Stevie left, making it possible for me

to finish my breakfast without having to worry about bodily injury.

A few minutes later Gwenny returned. B. C., who now was down on the floor, squealed with delight as she submitted herself to his embraces.

"One of these days," I predicted, "that little monster is going to strangle you. From the moment B. C. learned to walk he's been nothing but trouble."

"Wiggie!" Gwenny eyed me reproachfully. "Shame on you! You're the one who said we should always make a point of speaking kindly of others. Don't you remember? You said we should look for the positive side. You said that being tolerant is a sign of greatness, and . . ."

"Er . . . right." Had I said all that? "And believe me," I continued fervently, "I meant every word of it. Every word."

Ever since Gwenny first joined the family, I had made a point of sharing my vast reservoirs of knowledge with her. My daily lectures had covered a variety of subjects ranging from literature to nuclear power. Although I appreciated her rapt attention, I wished she wouldn't be quite so good at remembering what I had said. It was extremely irritating to be quoted later on as having said one thing or another.

"Being . . . eh . . . kind to others is definitely one of my top priorities," I assured her now. "Definitely." I cleared my throat. "That's why I wanted to extend a word of . . . uh . . . caution regarding B. C. I don't want you to get hurt, you know."

"Oh, Wiggie, how sweet of you!" Gwendolyn looked properly contrite. "I'm sorry I misjudged your intentions. I should have known you wouldn't purposely say anything bad about the baby."

That evening my pals and I were lined up on the back porch watching the sun go down. It had been a hot day, and even now it was still oppressively warm.

The pickup with its camper top, which held most of our stuff, was parked in the driveway. Mr. C. was going to drive that, with Stevie as passenger. The rest of us were riding in the station wagon with Mrs. C.

A few minutes before, the whole family had gone into town for dinner. For once everything was quiet.

Winston was the first one to break the silence.

"You know, it feels kind of funny to leave all this."

Josh rubbed his nose. "I know what you mean. This is the only place I've ever lived."

"Same here."

"I guess that goes for all of us," I said.

Gwenny wiped away a tear with her paw. "I'll sure miss the Bowers," she said, "especially Kathy." She sniffled. "But at least we'll come back again."

"Not until next year."

"Yep. Twelve whole months."

"Three hundred sixty-five days."

There was another prolonged silence. I looked at the familiar surroundings. It would be a long time before I saw them again. A lump began to form in my throat, and all of a sudden I wished I didn't have to move. What if Moscow turned out to be a terrible place to live? What if . . . ? I shuddered. What if something happened on the way and we didn't even get there? What if . . . ?

"Isn't that right, Wiggie?"

I jumped. "Uh . . . what?"

"As long as I have you to look after me," Gwendolyn repeated patiently, "I don't have to worry. You always know what to do."

Those words and her blue, trusting eyes brought me back to reality. I took a deep breath and straightened my shoulders. She was right, of course. I couldn't back out now. Everyone depended on me.

As was often the case these days, my thoughts went to my noble pioneer ancestors. Not only had they braved the storms of the Atlantic Ocean and adjusted to the customs and language of a strange country, they had also crossed the great plains under the harshest and most primitive conditions. Had they, I wondered now, ever regretted the decision to leave their home? Probably, but of course, I would never really know.

At this point in my reflections I was struck by a new idea. How could the story of my own heroic journey best be preserved for future generations? For the next few minutes I mulled over this most interesting problem. . . .

Now it was almost dark. A few stars twinkled in the sky. I decided that on this occasion a few well-chosen words might be appropriate. After all, this was an important turning point in our lives.

"Friends," I began solemnly, "fellow citizens." I looked around to make sure I had everyone's attention. "As you know, we are about to embark on a journey into the unknown. Like the early settlers, we will travel through areas where no white man has ever been before. We will . . ."

"But, Wiggie . . ."

I frowned disapprovingly at Gwendolyn. Did she always have to interrupt me just as I was warming up to my subject?

"What is it, Gwenny?"

"Well." Her face had a puzzled expression. "If no

white man has ever been there before, how will we get through? I mean, there won't be any roads for us to drive on, will there? And what if we run out of gas?"

"Eh . . ." I cleared my throat. "Certainly there are roads." Why did she always take everything I said so literally? This habit of hers was most irritating. "What I said was . . . uh . . . merely a figure of speech."

I tried to remember what else I had planned to say, but the unwelcome interruption had blanked it from my mind.

"Just . . . uh . . . remember one thing," I added in conclusion. "This will always be our true home." I paused. "By itself a house is just a house. It's your family, your loved ones, who make it a home. As long as we have each other, we'll feel at home no matter where we are."

It was evident by the silence that ensued that everybody was impressed by my words.

"I never thought I'd say this, Wiggie," Winston said finally, "but for once you're right. What's important is that we still have each other."

Gwendolyn looked adoringly at me. "I don't know how you do it, Wiggie," she said, "but you always manage to say the right thing at the right time."

I sighed. How very true.

"You were absolutely brilliant. I'm so glad I belong to this family. I don't know what I'd do if you were moving away and I'd never see you again. You're simply wonderful, Wiggie."

"I know," I said.

# SIX

"**W**iggie!"

The sound came from far away, interrupting my dream. But not for long. Soon I was back to where I had overpowered the outlaw by knocking him to the ground. I stood over him, my teeth at his throat, listening to him plead for mercy. . . .

"Wiggie, wake up!"

This time I recognized Gwendolyn's voice. I opened my eyes a fraction. "Huh?" I murmured. "What's up?"

"We're stopping for lunch."

I could feel the car slow down and then come to a standstill. "Hey," Josh exclaimed, "look at all those picnic tables."

The mention of food made my gastric juices come to life. My empty stomach made a loud gurgling sound, reminding me of how long it had been since we had had breakfast. I didn't mind eating at 4:00 A.M., as long as I was fed again at the usual hour, which was around seven. But today, once we were on the road, seven o'clock had come and gone with B. C. asleep, strapped in his car seat, Cilla likewise curled up and dead to the world, and Mrs. C. humming along to the music from the radio as she kept the car going at a steady sixty-five miles per hour.

Now Mrs. C. turned off the engine. In the ensuing silence, she sighed deeply. "Thank goodness! I was beginning to think that we'd never find a rest stop." Groaning, she eased herself out of the car while Cilla helped B. C.

A moment later the pickup with Mr. C. and Stevie pulled up. Mrs. C. and Cilla got out the coolers and began to set up the food on one of the tables.

"Stevie, can you let Winston out of the car?" Mrs. C. grabbed B. C. by the shirt before he had a chance to head for the highway.

Abandoning his handstand, Stevie reluctantly

sauntered over to the car. "You want the cats out, too?"

"Well . . ."

"Sure, let them out." That was Mr. C. "They won't go anywhere as long as there's food around. Besides, it's too hot for them in there."

A while later I had swallowed the last morsel of my Feline Feast. Licking my chops in satisfaction, I moved a little closer to Cilla's legs. A piece of her ham sandwich, I decided now, would be just the thing to round off my meal.

"I wonder how far we've come," Winston rumbled, looking around. "Do you think we're still in Virginia?"

"Well," I replied, "either that, or in a neighboring state. Judging by the presence of picnic tables, we're still in a fairly civilized area. Later on, we'll no doubt have to enjoy our meals in more primitive surroundings."

My attention was suddenly caught by an aroma that was distinctly familiar. I sniffed appreciatively. There was no mistaking the smell of fried chicken.

It didn't take me long to discover where it came from, either. At a nearby table a fat woman in shorts and a skinny man in blue jeans were about to enjoy their lunch.

47

I wandered casually in the general direction of the couple. After positioning myself in the shade of a tree, I wondered whether a direct begging approach would have the desired result. There was, of course, the remote possibility that these people didn't like cats.

I had hardly finished the thought when the man got up from the table and went to his car. By a stroke of incredible luck the wind chose that very moment to blow several paper plates across the grass. Immediately, the woman left her seat to retrieve them.

Without wasting any time, I made a daring leap up on the table. Quickly, I grabbed a large piece of juicy chicken from the container. Then, like a flash, I hit the ground again. The whole operation took about three seconds—a new personal record. Initially I had planned to take refuge under our car to enjoy my snack. But a startled exclamation from the woman forced me to change direction and head for the rest rooms instead.

As soon as I got inside I was struck by the utter lack of hiding places. The only possibility seemed to be a narrow door at the far wall, which was not quite shut. With the chicken still clamped between my teeth, I managed to pry the door open and squeeze inside. It was not a moment too soon.

"He went in here," I heard the woman say shrilly. "I saw him. It was a big, fat, ugly cat."

*Well!* I was shocked by her choice of adjectives. How *dare* she. And just who did she think she looked like herself? Miss America?

Now I heard heavy footsteps. "Don't see nobody here, Dora. Are you sure it was a cat?"

"Of course, I'm sure. You think I don't know what a cat looks like? Take my word for it, it was the most obese creature I've ever laid eyes on."

There she went again! Automatically, I bared my teeth and hissed.

"Did you hear that?" Her voice went up one octave.

Realizing that the door was still slightly ajar, I managed to pull it shut with one paw. The woman must have heard the click because almost immediately the knob turned.

"He's in there. I told you." The handle moved again.

More footsteps. Then Stevie's voice. "Nope."

"But I saw him just a minute ago." Cilla sounded worried. "He couldn't . . ."

"Looking for your cat, are you?"

"Er . . . yes. Have you seen him?"

"Have we?" The woman neighed like a horse. "Did you hear that, Alvin? They want to know if we've seen their cat. You bet your bottom dollar we have, honey. He's right in here." Again she rattled the handle. "And I guess that's where he'll stay, since the door is locked."

This piece of news came as a shock to me. Locked? The door was locked?

"Don't look like there's a key anywhere, either," Alvin said helpfully. "Guess you'll have to . . ."

"Stole some of our chicken, that's what he did," the woman interrupted brusquely. "You folks should keep an eye on your pets if you insist on letting them run loose. Besides, there's a sign outside that says . . ."

"Wiggie?" Now Cilla was by the door. "Wiggie-pooh, are you in there?"

My only thought at that moment was the frightening possibility of having to stay locked up in that dark rest-room closet forever. Forgetting even the plump chicken breast at my feet, I opened my mouth.

*"Mia-u-w!"* I cried.

"What if the caretaker hadn't been home?" Gwenny said when I was safely back in the station wagon. "You'd still be in there."

I shuddered at the thought. The three hours I had spent in the closet had been long enough for me.

51

Good thing that loud-mouthed woman hadn't stayed around. The way she had carried on about the one measly piece of chicken I'd helped myself to, you'd think it was her last crumb of food. Yet I knew for a fact that there had been at least half a dozen chicken breasts left in the container.

"Weren't you scared, Wiggie?" Gwenny asked.

"Of course not." I gave her a reassuring smile. "There was nothing in there to be scared of. Just a couple of buckets and some brooms." Stifling a yawn, I added, "I knew all along they'd get me out, of course. It was just a matter of time."

"Well"—Winston guffawed—"if they hadn't, we could always have picked you up on our way back. Next year, that is." His whole body shook with laughter.

"Very funny." I gave him a frosty stare. Sometimes his sense of humor was really warped. Then I turned my back to him and curled up against Cilla's duffel bag. A moment later I was fast asleep.

My unfortunate experience had really worn me out. I slept like a log and didn't even wake up when, hours later, we drove up in front of a motel. In fact, I didn't open my eyes until Cilla carried me inside and put me down on the bed.

"When can we go in the pool?" Stevie asked.

"Not until after dinner." Mrs. C. looked critically at him. "And if you want to eat, you'd better get another shirt on."

"What's wrong with this one?"

"It's dirty."

"I don't see any dirt."

Cilla made a face at him. "That's probably because there isn't a clean spot left to compare with. Why do you always have to look like a bum?"

"Look who's talking. The stuff around your eyes makes you look like a clown."

"Mom," Cilla wailed, "did you hear that?"

Mrs. C. sighed. "I'm leaving now. Of course, if you two would rather stay here and bicker . . ."

After everybody was gone we watched a game show on television. Mrs. C. had left the TV on for us, just the way she sometimes does at home. None of the contestants was very bright. In spite of this, one of them somehow managed to win both a car and a trip for two to Hawaii. When that was over they showed an old "Cosby Show," which was pretty boring.

Since tonight quite possibly would be the last one spent in civilized surroundings, I had hoped to be able to explore the motel premises. Unfortunately, an earlier attempt to sneak out the door had been cut short by Mr. C. He was still in a bad mood because of the delay at the rest area, which for some reason he considered to be my fault.

Now a sudden knock on the door was followed by the sound of a key in the lock. A short, stubby maid carrying a stack of towels disappeared into the bathroom, leaving the door ajar behind her.

Josh and I looked at each other. Two seconds later we were racing down the hallway. When the maid came back out we were already halfway down the stairs.

"Wow!" Josh exclaimed as we collapsed in the grass behind a cluster of shrubs. "That was close."

We lay there for a while, waiting for our breathing to get back to normal. Then we padded leisurely across the lawn to the brightly lit pool. Half a dozen deck chairs with colorful plastic webbing were scattered around the pool area. With the exception of a man who was floating on his back in the water, it was completely deserted.

Josh looked around. "Where is everybody?"

"Having dinner, I guess. Or getting ready for bed. It's getting late." I stared intently at the figure in the water. "Have you noticed how that guy isn't moving at all?"

"He could be sleeping. His eyes are closed."

"No way. He'd sink like a stone."

We watched for another while.

"Maybe," I suggested, "somebody just dumped him there."

"You mean he might be dead?"

I shrugged. "Not necessarily. He could be unconscious. Probably the victim of a saloon brawl."

"There aren't any saloons around here. This is a motel, remember? All they have is a regular restaurant."

We moved closer to the edge of the pool. The man, who was wearing blue-and-white swimming trunks, was now no more than six feet away. He still hadn't moved.

"You think he'll wake up soon?" Josh asked.

I shrugged again. "Who knows?"

I looked down into the green water. Something was lying on the bottom. I wondered if it belonged to the man.

Now Josh nudged me with his paw. "Let's go."

"The sheriff should probably be notified," I said.

"Everybody is in bed."

"The Carters aren't," I reminded him. "They should be here any time now."

"All the more reason for us to leave," Josh said nervously. "We're not supposed to be here."

Unfortunately, he was right. Still, I hesitated.

"Well," Josh said finally, "I'm leaving."

"How are you going to get in?"

"That's easy. I'll wait in the hallway around the corner and sneak in as soon as they open the door."

After he had left I made my way over to the diving board, which would allow me a better view of the man in the water.

It was hard to believe that only this morning I had been sleeping in my familiar basket in the living room. Now, a mere fifteen hours later, I was faced with a situation that most likely ought to be investigated by the sheriff.

I was proud of the way I was able to calmly assess the situation. Fortunately, I had inherited the raw courage that had characterized my noble pioneer ancestors. Somebody had to keep an eye on the victim until the sheriff came. I was the obvious person to do it. It was as simple as that. The possibility existed that the outlaws who were responsible for the attack on this man would return.

I wondered idly what the reason might have been for knocking him out cold in the first place? Or—here my heart skipped a beat—was this perhaps the result of a gunfight?

But if the man in the water had been shot, then I should be able to spot where the bullet had gone in.

In order to get a closer look, I moved a little farther out on the diving board. Yes, I decided after a moment, there was a dark spot on his shoulder that might fit the bill. I put my paws around the edge of the board and craned my neck to make sure.

A second later I was trying frantically to regain my balance. Instead, I felt myself completely losing my grip. To my horror I was falling helplessly through the air, finally hitting the water with a splash. The water instantly closed over my head, and I was sucked down to the bottom of the pool.

# SEVEN

The first thing I noticed when I regained consciousness was that I was lying face down on something soft and fluffy. The second thing I noticed was that someone was squeezing my poor tummy.

Suddenly overcome by nausea, I opened my mouth and threw up. Then, completely exhausted, I sank back on the soft, fluffy thing, which, I realized now, was a folded bath towel.

"Well, well! I guess you're going to live, after all."

Tiredly, I wondered who was talking.

"Not very pleasant to swallow a lot of water, was it?" Strong hands turned me around and I looked into the face of the man who had been floating around in the pool. Well, at least he wasn't dead. Not that I really cared.

Now the man began to rub me with the towel, which immediately made me feel somewhat better.

"You sure made a big splash when you fell into the water, old fellow. Practically gave me a heart attack. When I opened my eyes and saw you sink to the bottom like a rock"—here he laughed out loud— "I didn't know what you were. I certainly had no idea you were an animal."

At that point I began to make gagging noises, and he quickly turned me over so I could throw up some more water.

"Then I decided to dive down to see what it was, and . . ." He laughed again. "Could hardly believe my eyes. I grabbed you by the scruff and, my goodness, were you heavy. After I got you out of the water and had a chance to look at you, I thought you were in the last stages of pregnancy. Ha, ha, ha. Then I realized I was wrong, of course, but frankly, old boy, even in your drenched state you strongly resembled an overinflated balloon."

Under normal circumstances I would have shown my resentment over these insults. Since circumstances were anything but normal and because I felt so rotten, I decided to let it pass.

As I was drifting off to sleep, I heard from far away the slamming of a door and the voices of Mrs. C. and Stevie. Moments later I was back in Cilla's familiar arms. There was a lot of explaining going on before I finally was carried inside.

Judging by the shocked expression on Winston's face when Cilla opened the door to our room, I must have looked pretty awful. Too exhausted by my ordeal for any conversation, I closed my eyes. I was asleep even before Cilla had finished tucking me into bed.

The next morning when I finally woke up, I still felt pretty bad. There was nothing wrong with my appetite, however. The rest of the family must have been up for hours, because they were almost ready to leave.

"And how is my poor baby today?" Cilla cooed while giving me my breakfast. "You really gave us a scare, Wiggie-pooh, did you know that?"

I sneezed a couple of times. I decided it was quite possible that I was coming down with pneumonia.

Mrs. C. must have had the same thought. She said worriedly, "We'd better give Wiggie some warm milk. The last thing we need is a sick cat on our hands."

Mr. C. glared at me. "Sick or not," he muttered, "the last thing we need is to have this *particular* cat on our hands. By God," he exploded suddenly, "one day on the road and not only does he steal other people's chicken and lock himself in a closet that doesn't have a key, delaying us for hours, but he then has the nerve to sneak out of the motel as soon as we turn our backs and get himself drowned in the swimming pool."

"Almost drowned, Dad," Cilla corrected him.

Stevie grinned while making one of his usual revolting sounds. "Maybe next time he'll do a better job of it," he commented hopefully. "Maybe there won't be anyone around to save him. He's too fat to swim, anyway."

Mr. C. glowered. "If I have anything to say, there won't be a next time. We'll take care of that this very morning." He smiled grimly.

I must still have been suffering from the aftereffects of my adventure, because no sooner was I put in the car than I fell asleep again. The next thing I knew, we were parked at the curb outside a store, and Cilla was carrying me inside. I managed to get a brief glimpse of the name on the door. In large gold lettering it said *Eddie's Pet Emporium*. I had no idea what we were doing there, unless perhaps it was to buy me a nice warm sweater so I wouldn't catch pneumonia.

A stout, balding man with glasses came up and asked what he could do for us.

"Well." Mr. C. glared vindictively in my direction. "What we *really* need is a straitjacket, but I guess that's too much to hope for. . . ." He sighed regretfully.

*Straitjacket?* Now, wait a minute . . .

". . . so I guess we'll settle for a harness of some kind, if you have that. . . ."

Now began the most humiliating experience of my life, as I was unmercifully squeezed into all kinds of contraptions, none of which seemed to fit.

At the end of the session, the stout man was breathing heavily. He pulled a handkerchief out of his pocket and wiped his forehead. "I'm terribly sorry," he gasped, "but none of the cat harnesses seems to fit him. Not even the extra-extra-large. Maybe what we should try are some of the smaller ones for dogs. . . ."

More humiliation as another array of leather straps were pulled over my head and around my tummy.

Finally, the man threw up his hands. "I'm terribly sorry," he said again. "The poodle sizes are too small and the ones that are made for medium-sized dogs are too big." Again he wiped his face with the handkerchief. "And I really don't know what else to suggest, except perhaps a regular collar and a leash."

"What took you so long in there?" Josh wanted to know. "What did they . . ." Here he stopped. "Hey, guys, look at Wiggie. He has a collar."

"That's right," I said offhandedly. "Mrs. C. was going to buy me a sweater, except the store didn't have any. So, I got a collar instead." I touched it with my paw. "Handtooled leather with metal studs. The very latest in Western fashion."

"Oh, yeah?" Winston sounded skeptical. "I bet I know the *real* reason why they bought you a collar. It's for the next time you decide to fall into the pool, ha, ha. It makes it easier to pull you out."

I eyed him coldly. "For your information, it certainly has more style than your choke chain."

"Well, I think you look absolutely wonderful, Wiggie," Gwenny assured me. "So rugged."

I thought so myself. Mr. C. had at first picked out a red plastic collar with multicolored rhinestones all over it—as a kind of revenge, I guess. Fortunately, Cilla had put her foot down and I had ended up with this one instead.

"Say, Wiggie." Josh sounded curious. "What exactly happened last night? Why did you jump into the pool?"

"Last night?" I began to rearrange the blanket in my basket. Unfortunately, I hadn't had any time to think about what to tell them. "Oh, you mean last night!" I settled in as comfortably as I could. "Well," I began, "after you left I kept on watching the guy who was floating around in the pool. He still wasn't moving at all and his eyes remained closed. As I was sitting there, the thought struck me that maybe he was . . . uh . . . sick or something. Maybe he had fainted. So"—I licked my paw—"I decided to see if I could revive him."

"Revive him?" Winston looked puzzled. "How were you going to do that?"

"Well," I said, "my idea was to splash some water on his face to see if that would wake him up. Then, as I looked at the diving board, I decided it might be more effective if I jumped in from there. Logically, this would create a much larger splash. So that's exactly what I did. And," I added modestly, "it worked."

Gwenny had been listening with her mouth open. "You mean he really did wake up?"

"That's right. Unfortunately, when he flipped around and began to swim, he also managed to push me under water. Not on purpose, of course. I don't even think he saw me until I started coughing and spluttering. Since I was taken completely by surprise, I swallowed a lot of water. Anyway, he grabbed hold of me and pulled me out. And that's when Cilla and everybody else showed up."

Now Winston started chuckling. "Wiggie, old pal, you looked just like a drowned rat. But I still don't understand what made you jump into the pool in the first place. I know how much you hate water."

"For your information," I replied stiffly, "my sole concern was for the welfare of that poor man. The fact that I am not overly fond of water was, at that moment, of no importance whatsoever."

"Oh, Wiggie," Gwenny said admiringly, "you always think of others first."

How right she was. But then, compassion was just one of my countless virtues.

"We should all learn from you."

"Well." I gave Winston a meaningful glance. "Not everyone is willing to put his life on the line to help those who are in need. In this case," I added, "it turned out that this man really had passed out while he was floating in the pool. For years he has suffered from a bad heart."

In spite of himself, Josh was impressed. "You mean, you may actually have saved his life?"

I shrugged. "I guess that's what it amounts to. Although," I continued modestly, "I did only what any other caring, upright citizen would have done."

Drowsiness was once more overtaking me. "And now if you'll excuse me," I said, yawning, "I'd better get some shut-eye. Mrs. C. is afraid I might develop pneumonia as a result of my adventure." As I curled up I was reminded of the leather collar I was wearing. Like me, it was truly rugged, befitting the lifestyle of the West. I shuddered as I remembered how close I had come to having to wear a harness. Not to mention the flashy rhinestone collar. I really didn't know which one would have been worse.

# EIGHT

"I must admit," Mrs. C. commented, "that it's a lot prettier along these back roads than it is along the highway."

Cilla, who was reading a book about our fifty states, said, "Did you know that Highway forty was one of the very first highways built in this country? And that Indiana is one of the main producers of turkeys?"

So far I had been listening with half an ear to their conversation. Now the word *turkey* got my attention. "Indiana sounds just like my kind of state," I murmured to my pals in the back of the car. "I wouldn't mind having turkey for dinner every night."

Josh opened his mouth to yawn. "You'd get tired of it after a while," he predicted. "Remember when Mrs. C. bought those two cases of tuna for practically nothing because the cans were dented? And how we got to eat the leftovers from all the different tuna dishes she made? Boy, did I get sick and tired of tuna!"

"Indiana," I mused. "A rather revealing name, wouldn't you say?"

"What do you mean, revealing?"

"I'm referring to our red-skinned brothers, of course. What else? Obviously we're approaching Indian territory. I suspect that from now on we'll have to do without some of the comforts and conveniences we've been accustomed to. Motels, for example. It could be that tonight we'll have to rest our weary bodies at a stagecoach stop of some kind."

"That's fine with me," Winston rumbled, "as long as I get my dinner."

"Talking about dinner, my favorite food is sardines." Gwendolyn, like the rest of us, was looking out the rear window at the passing landscape. "And whipped cream." She sighed. "I just *love* whipped cream."

"How about a nice, juicy T-bone steak?" Winston licked his chops. "Or a large ham bone with lots of meat left on it?"

All this talk about food made my stomach growl. Today we hadn't even stopped for lunch. I'd had my usual bowl of dry nuggets, of course, but eating in the car wasn't much fun.

As if she had read my thoughts, Cilla said complainingly, "Mom, it's almost dinnertime. Aren't we going to stop somewhere and eat? I need to get out and stretch, too. My legs keep on falling asleep. And B. C. wants to get out and crawl around." She reached out and tickled his tummy. "Don't you, baby?"

Soon after, we pulled off the road onto an open grassy space. The Carters had submarine sandwiches, potato salad, and Jell-O for dinner. Winston, Josh, Gwendolyn, and I had dry dog food.

"I don't understand it," Mrs. C. said helplessly. "I could have *sworn* I packed another bag of cat food."

"You left it on the kitchen table," Stevie said.

"I did? Then why didn't you say something?"

"I thought you were giving it to the people who were going to rent our house."

"The *Browns* . . . ? For goodness sake, Stevie, why would I do that? They don't even *have* a cat."

"But they have two poodles, don't they? They've probably finished the whole bag by now."

"Yuk!" Josh made a gagging sound. "I'm not going to eat this stuff. It tastes like sawdust."

Unfortunately, he was right. After sampling the dog food myself, I was beginning to feel queasy.

"Here." Josh pushed his food over to Winston. "Be my guest." He turned his attention to the water bowl.

"You can have mine, too." I wondered if I was going to be sick.

"What's the matter with you guys?" Winston seemed genuinely surprised. "This is really delicious. My favorite flavor, too. Beef nuggets with moist chicken pieces in the center." He scratched his chest noisily. "And it's loaded with protein and vitamins."

Gwendolyn hadn't even touched hers. "Sorry, Winston," she said apologetically, "but it smells kind of funny."

"It does?" Winston continued to look puzzled. "Guess I'll have to eat it all, then. But don't complain if you're still hungry."

"Mom, the cats aren't eating. I told you they wouldn't like dog food." Cilla reached for the bread. "I'll make a sandwich and split it between them."

71

"What for?" Mr. C. muttered uncharitably. "Skipping a meal never hurt anyone. Just look at them, Wiggie especially. So fat he can hardly move."

Shocked by this unfair description of my body, I bared my teeth and hissed at him. Then I eased myself closer to Cilla. She was spreading a generous amount of mayonnaise on the bread before topping it with thick slices of baloney and cheese.

Soon I was chomping away on my share of the submarine sandwich. It really hit the spot. Generously, I decided to forgive Mr. C. his remarks. He was probably just nervous because of the new job that was awaiting him in Idaho.

My hunger finally appeased, I tended to my grooming while admiring the peaceful surroundings. A cluster of trees, a lush green meadow scattered with wildflowers, a red barn in the distance. Indeed, I thought approvingly, Mrs. C. had chosen the perfect place for our picnic dinner.

Now she began to put the food away while Mr. C., with a satisfied grunt, stretched out on his back in the grass. Cilla and Stevie were throwing a Frisbee to each other. B. C., lying on his blanket, waved his rubber toy in the air while gurgling happily.

Feeling the need for a little exercise to aid my digestion, I headed for the nearest cluster of trees.

The evening sun was pleasantly warm on my back. Added to the satisfaction of having a full stomach and nice fresh air in my lungs, it made my contentment complete. This, I decided, was life at its best.

As I proceeded into an area shaded by trees, I enjoyed the softness of the green moss under my paws. It was almost like walking on air. There was certainly a lot to be said for the wilderness.

Unfortunately this feeling of contentment was short-lived, as I was startled by a sudden rustling noise from among the bushes. I stopped and listened. What had caused it? At first all was quiet. Then I had a fleeting glimpse of a large moving shadow followed by a strange swishing sound.

With the infallible instinct that no doubt had characterized my pioneer ancestors, I knew at once what it was. Indians! The swishing sound could only have come from an arrow, which must have passed over my head, since I was still unharmed. How utterly careless of me not to have foreseen that something like this might happen. After all, here we were in the state of Indiana, which, judging by its name, could well be the cradle of all the Indian tribes on this continent.

Even as these reflections went through my mind, I turned and raced back in the direction I had come from. Straining my limbs to the uttermost, it was only a matter of seconds before I had reached the pickup. Fortunately the back door was wide open, enabling me to execute one of my daring leaps into its dark interior.

Totally out of breath, I collapsed behind one of the boxes. I was pretty sure the enemy had not had time to see where I had gone.

"What on earth has gotten into Wiggie?" There was astonishment in Cilla's voice. "I've never seen him run like that before."

The realization that the rest of the family were still out there, in danger of being attacked by the Indians, hit me like a ton of bricks. Still gasping for breath, I managed to sit up and peek over the top of the box. I could see Mr. and Mrs. C., apparently unaware of the impending danger, playing with B. C. Winston was nowhere in sight, but both Josh and Gwendolyn were coming toward the pickup.

I raised myself a little higher and looked in the direction of the bushes. There, cheered on by Stevie, a large black-and-white cow came ambling along. She was contentedly chewing on a mouthful of grass. Each time her tail hit her hindquarters it made a swishing noise.

"Hey, Wiggie, what's the matter? Did the cow scare you?" Josh jumped up on the tailgate. "Or were you practicing for the Boston marathon, ha, ha?"

Refusing to respond in kind, I said haughtily, "Has it ever occurred to you that lying around in the car all day, day after day, could seriously impede your health? As it happens, I was merely taking steps to ensure my continued physical fitness."

"Oh, yeah?" Disbelief was written all over Josh's face. "Is that why you were running like a scared rabbit?"

I stared coldly at him. "For your information, old pal, I finished my sixty-yard sprint in only five and a half seconds. Top that if you can."

Gwenny said admiringly, "I think the whole concept is wonderful, Wiggie. That's what we all should be doing."

I blinked. "Uh . . . we should?"

"Of course. We all need exercise. We could race each other. Maybe even do some high jumps. Wouldn't that be fun?"

I shuddered. Just the thought made me tired. "Eh . . . sure thing, Gwenny. That's a great idea."

"We could start tonight as soon as we get to the motel. Or," she amended, "the stagecoach stop."

Josh snickered. "Do you really think we'll get a chance to go outside after what happened last night?"

"Well, we could always run around the room," Gwendolyn suggested brightly.

I shuddered again. Hopefully, she would have forgotten all about it by tonight. Personally, I wished I didn't have to move another muscle until we arrived in Idaho.

# NINE

"Look, now you're cheating again."

"I am not."

"You are, too. You used the ten of hearts a little while ago and now you're using it again."

"Hah! You're just saying that because you're losing."

"That's not true," Cilla said accusingly. "How do you expect me to win when you're cheating all the time?" She slammed her cards down on the seat. "I'm not going to play with you ever again."

"See if I care." Stevie stuffed a handful of corn chips into his mouth and began to chew with his mouth open. The crunching noise grated on my ears.

"Why can't he ride in the pickup like he's supposed to?" Josh said irritably.

"Mr. C. probably couldn't take it any longer."

"They should have locked him up in the back of the truck to begin with," Winston said vindictively. "That way he wouldn't be able to bug anyone." Winston was still smarting from being hit by Stevie's remote-control helicopter. Fortunately, one of the rotor blades broke shortly afterward, when it smashed into the dashboard.

I sighed and stared out the window. "It won't be long now before we reach the prairie," I said. "And the buffaloes."

"Do you think we'll see cowboys riding around?" Gwenny asked.

I nodded. "Most likely. And it could be that we'll all have to have our dinner under the stars tonight. Cooked over the campfire."

Winston grunted. "You mean there won't be any more restaurants around?"

"I'm afraid not." I shook my head. "No restaurants. No motels."

Josh said accusingly, "That's what you said last

night, too, Wiggie. And the night before. And where did we sleep? In motels, that's where."

I decided to ignore his remark. No one had been more surprised than I to find modern conveniences this far west. After all, we had now been on the road for four whole days.

For the first time I noticed that we had left the highway and were slowly driving down a street lined with businesses and stores.

"Here's one, Mom," Cilla said suddenly.

"Where?"

"Over there." She pointed.

Josh opened one eye. "One what?"

"Supermarket," Gwenny informed him. "We need to buy diapers and milk."

Josh gave me a meaningful nudge. "I thought you said we were finally past civilization," he said with a snicker. "Then how come we have this giant supermarket right in front of us?"

I gave him a haughty stare. "For your information," I replied coldly, "I never said there wouldn't be any *stores* around. I was talking about restaurants and motels. Believe it or not, stores did exist even a hundred years ago. It's only logical that they have grown larger and . . . eh . . . more efficient since then."

Soon Mrs. C. had maneuvered the car into the parking lot and turned off the engine.

"Stevie," she said over her shoulder, "you take Winston for a walk while Cilla and I go inside."

"What?" Stevie sat up, looking highly insulted. "Why me? Why do I always have to walk that dumb dog?"

"It's your turn," Cilla reminded him. "I did it last time." She flashed her brother a triumphant smile.

"But I need to buy some things."

Mrs. C. lifted a protesting B. C. out of his seat. "Just let me know what you need and I'll get it for you."

Stevie hesitated. "Uh . . . I want a . . . uh . . . candy bar."

"You already had one today. That's enough."

"I need some other things, too."

"Like what?" Cilla raised her eyebrows. "You already have chips and pop."

Stevie reached for the leash. "I *hate* walking that stupid dog," he muttered.

Mrs. C. gave him a stern look.

"He'd better watch it," Winston growled.

I was struck by a brilliant idea. "Why don't you bite him when no one is watching? I bet that if he tells, nobody will believe him."

Stevie made one last try. "Do I *have* to walk him?"

"Yes, you have to. Take Winston over to that grassy area and stay there until we get back."

After everyone had left, peace reigned. Gwenny curled up and went to sleep. Josh and I took the opportunity to stretch our legs by moving up to the front of the car. For a while we played tag with the mascot that was tied to the rearview mirror. After we tired of that, we climbed into the back seat and helped ourselves to some of Stevie's corn chips.

Both of us were on the floor looking for crumbs when we heard the back door open.

"I knew it," Josh said. "I *knew* it. He's back with Winston already."

The door slammed shut again.

"Say, Winston," I began, while climbing back up on the seat, "did you . . ."

I left the sentence hanging in the air as soon as I realized that Winston wasn't there. But then who had opened the door? And—I scratched my head, puzzled—where was Gwenny?

A sudden muffled cry made me look out the window. Walking away from the car was a little girl with short blond hair. And clutched in her arms was a long-haired white cat.

The cat was Gwendolyn.

"Don't get in, Winston," I said urgently, as soon as Stevie had opened the door. "Stay right where you are."

"Uh . . . why?" Winston stopped, looking bewildered. Stevie tried to urge Winston into the car with his knee.

"It's Gwenny," Josh said. "She's gone. Somebody took her."

"*Took* her?" Now Winston seemed even more mystified. "What do you mean, *took* her?"

"It means she's been kidnapped," I said impatiently. "A little girl just took her out of the car while everybody was in the store. She carried her away in that direction." I showed him. "Winston, you have to find her."

"Mom," Stevie complained. "Winston won't get in."

Mrs. C., who had just emerged from the supermarket, sighed. "Then lift him in, for heaven's sake." She was trying to get B. C. to stop crying while at the same time arranging the bags up front. "Cilla, hurry up and find his bottle. It has to be on the floor somewhere."

Stevie let go of the leash while trying to get a grip on Winston.

"Now!" I hissed. "Run!"

Winston extracted himself from Stevie's grasp and took off across the parking lot. As luck would have it, his freedom was rather short-lived, since he had the misfortune to run into Mr. C.

Watching him being collared again, Josh said worriedly, "What do we do now, Wiggie?"

For once, I couldn't think of anything. "We'll have to wait until they find out that Gwenny is gone, I guess."

"But they won't know what happened to her."

"I know that." That's why I had counted on Winston to lead them in the right direction.

Now the car door opened and a mortified Winston was unceremoniously shoved inside. After a cursory glance at Josh and me, Mr. C. shut the door, and he and Stevie started walking back to the pickup.

"Did you see that?" Josh said agitatedly, "He didn't even *notice* that Gwenny is missing. What if we leave without her?"

My blood ran cold at the possibility. Somehow, I felt personally responsible for Gwendolyn. No way were we leaving without her. Not if I could help it.

Looking wildly around, I saw that Mrs. C. was already fastening her seatbelt. Cilla was about to get in. Her door was still wide open. Without hesitating, I jumped out of my basket and, like lightning, I flew past Cilla. Once I hit the ground, I stopped for a moment to get my bearings. Then I took off in the direction I had seen the little girl disappear to.

Even as I took a shortcut under a van, I heard Cilla calling, "Wiggie, wait! Where are you going?"

Soon she was joined by Mrs. C.

"Wiggie!"

"Come on, Wiggie-pooh!"

"Dad! Wiggie got out. Did you see him?"

"For heaven's sake," Mr. C. said irritably, "is he gone, too? What's the matter with everybody?"

"Wiggie!"

I tried to blank out all the commotion while I sniffed around the cars. Taking the risk of being heard myself, I called, "Gwenny, where are you?"

When there was no response, I moved on to the next row of cars. I could see—not to mention smell—Stevie's dirty sneakers. Since I was hiding behind a wheel, he didn't see me. Even so, I knew it was only a matter of time before I was caught.

But first I had to find Gwenny.

"Gwendolyn!" I called. "Gwenny!"

Amidst all the noise the family was making, I thought I heard a faint cry.

Immediately I stopped and held my breath. Had I only imagined it? "Gwenny, is that you?" I wondered anxiously whether I really would be able to find her before someone found me. "Gwenny?" Again there was a muffled cry. Then, all of a sudden, I spotted Gwendolyn's frightened face pressed against the front window of a beige sedan.

"Gwenny!" In a flash I was up on the hood. Inside

the car the little girl was sitting by herself in the driver's seat. She was eating a banana. Poor Gwenny was crouching on the dashboard.

"Wiggie!" Cilla called again. Then she saw me. "Oh, there you are, baby. Mom! Dad! I found him." To my horror, she was picking me up. Desperate at the thought that she wouldn't see Gwenny, I did something I had never ever done before: I scratched Cilla's arms.

"*Aaoo!*" With a startled cry she let go of me. Quickly, I moved out of her reach and started clawing at the window. Gwenny did the same from the inside while crying pitifully.

"Mom! Wiggie has gone crazy. He . . ." Cilla's jaw dropped. *"Gwenny!"*

Suddenly everyone was there.

"What on earth is Gwenny doing in that car?" asked Mr. C.

"Gwenny?" Mrs. C. looked confused. "That can't be her. She's still in our car."

"How do you know? Wiggie got out."

Cilla was licking the blood from her arms. "It's Gwenny, Mom," she said tearfully. "Don't you recognize her collar? That's why Wiggie scratched me. He didn't want to leave without her. And that's why he ran away. He was trying to find Gwenny."

Mr. C. had already opened the car door. "Would

86

you mind telling me what you are doing with our cat?" he said to the girl. Without waiting for her answer, he reached past her and grabbed Gwendolyn.

"It's *my* cat," the girl protested. "I found her."

"Oh, yeah?" Mr. C. said. "And just where did you find her?"

The girl took another bite of her banana. Now she seemed frightened. "I found her in a car."

"You mean you opened the door and took her?"

"She was lying in a basket," the girl repeated. "I found her."

Mr. C. sighed. "Well," he said, "you're not supposed to take things out of other people's cars, remember that."

For once I didn't even mind being carried by Stevie. I was so relieved it was all over.

"Wasn't that brave of Wiggie to try to find Gwenny?" Cilla said. "He must have seen the girl take her."

"Hey," Stevie said suddenly, "maybe that's why Winston ran off, too."

"What *I* want to know," said Mr. C., "is how come no one noticed that Gwenny was missing?"

I had never been more grateful to curl up in my familiar basket than I was then. Cilla insisted that

I get some kind of reward for finding Gwenny, so Mrs. C. went back into the store. Soon I was chomping away on creamed shrimp while Gwenny was eating chicken liver.

"You saved my life, Wiggie," she said for the fifth time. "You really did. How can I ever thank you?"

Feeling better already with something in my stomach, I replied modestly, "Oh, it was nothing. I was only doing my duty."

Actually, I was rather impressed myself by what I had done. With ancestors who risked their lives enforcing law and order in the Wild West, it was not surprising that I was displaying similar courage.

I was suddenly reminded of a James Bond movie I had watched recently. He, too, had saved the life of a girl who had been kidnapped. Maybe, some day, someone would make a movie about my heroic adventures.

"That was such a brave thing to do, Wiggie." Gwenny looked adoringly at me with her large blue eyes.

Modestly, I looked down at the floor.

"Really, Wiggie, there's no one like you."

I sighed.

"I know that," I said.

# TEN

Bang! Bang, bang, bang! Bang! Bang!

The floor of the saloon was suddenly littered with bodies.

Bang! Sensing that someone was behind him, the sheriff spun around. Another shot and the gun flew out of the hand of one of the villains.

"Nice going," Winston murmured, encouragingly. "Keep it up."

Bang! Bang!

Gwendolyn, who had buried her face in a pillow,

said in a muffled voice, "Tell me when they've stopped shooting."

"They won't until the end," Josh informed her cheerfully. Without taking his eyes off the screen, he nudged her with his paw. "You should watch it. It's a great movie."

It was one of John Wayne's earlier Westerns and it was pretty good.

Now the only one left for the sheriff to deal with was the number-one bad guy. As usual they were facing each other in the middle of a dusty street. And as usual it took John Wayne about thirty seconds to dispose of him. After that they showed the grateful townspeople and, of course, the beautiful girl throwing herself around the sheriff's neck.

When it was over Winston sighed deeply. "Those were the good old days," he said wistfully.

"Yep." Josh stretched and yawned. "Gone forever."

"Don't be so sure," I said.

Josh stifled another yawn. "Have you heard any gunshots around here?"

"This is a motel," I pointed out, "not a saloon."

"Exactly," he retorted. "*You're* the one who keeps on telling us we're finally getting out to the real Wild West. And where are we? In another boring motel. That's why I'm telling you that the good old days are gone forever."

"There's a bar downstairs," I protested.

"That doesn't mean anything. It's still a motel. How many guests do you think they would get if there *really* was a saloon here? With gunfights and stuff like that? They might as well close down the place."

Although I totally disagreed with what he said, I decided not to argue the point. During the last hour or so before we reached the motel, I had seen enough evidence to convince me that we finally were in the real West. My pals had all been asleep at the time. Since I didn't want to get Gwenny upset, I hadn't even told them about it.

We had, for one thing, passed several large signs with names like *The Buffalo Ranch, The Last Stand Corral,* and *The Big Horn Saloon.* Displayed over the front door of the saloon was the head of a steer with giant horns.

No, I decided grimly, there was no sense fooling ourselves. In spite of the seemingly peaceful surroundings right here inside the motel, we'd better prepare ourselves for the rugged reality of what was around us.

I looked at my pals, hoping that they wouldn't have to experience the Wild West the hard way.

As usual, the Carters had left the television on for us, and, as usual, Winston had his eyes glued to the screen. For some reason he thinks commercials are interesting. "Quiet, guys," he said now. "I can't hear what they're saying."

I noticed that Gwenny had gone to sleep. Maybe that's what I should do, too, even though I wasn't particularly tired. Unfortunately, I was prompted by my strong sense of duty to try to find a way out of this room. I needed to do some scouting around to determine what kind of dangers might be awaiting us.

Unexpectedly, a key rattled in the lock. A moment later Stevie came stomping in. He started digging for something in one of the bags, tossing clothes in a pile on the floor in the process.

My spirits rose at the sight of the open door, which practically invited me to step outside. For a moment I was tempted to ask Josh to join me. Then, thinking of his safety, I decided I'd better go on my own. It was up to me to meet whatever dangers were there.

Both Winston and Josh were engrossed in the television. Fortunately, Stevie had his back to the bed. Silently I jumped down onto the floor. Then, like a shadow, I slipped out the door, not stopping until I was safely hidden by a large planter that was standing in a corner.

A few minutes later Stevie appeared, slamming the door behind him. He walked noisily past me down the stairs. As soon as he was out of sight I moved from my hiding place.

The downstairs hall was deserted. I stopped, undecided. Which way was out?

A sudden whiff of something delectable made my mouth water. I licked my chops. As if drawn by a magnet, I followed the tempting smells, which became stronger as I came closer to the kitchen. Eventually, the only thing that separated me from all the goodies was a pair of louvered half-doors that ended about eight inches above the floor.

Very cautiously, I padded forward and peeked underneath the door. The only person in the kitchen at the moment was a man dressed in white with a tall cook's hat on his head. He was busy transferring juicy T-bone steaks from the grill to two dinner plates. I noticed that the steaks were almost as large as the plates.

Overcome by this heavenly sight, I could hear my poor growling tummy. How could I get my paws on one of those steaks?

While trying to come up with a workable plan, I

flattened myself behind a large, round metal container inside the door. Now the cook placed a large foil-wrapped baked potato on each of the plates. Then he took down two other plates from a large stack on the shelf. These he loaded with fish fillets swimming in butter, mashed potatoes, and tender green peas. I almost passed out from the heavenly aroma that wafted through the air.

After what seemed like an eternity, the cook finally turned his back on the plates. Humming a tune in a deep bass voice, he first lifted a pot off the stove. Then he went to the other end of the kitchen to get something out of a cabinet.

Unable to restrain myself any longer, I made a daring leap up onto the counter. Soon my teeth were buried in the thickest of the steaks. Somehow the situation seemed familiar. It was a moment before I remembered the barbecued chicken at the rest stop.

I now experienced a moment of sheer panic as I discovered that the steak was so heavy I couldn't lift it. Refusing to let this keep me from my appointed task, I proceeded to drag it behind me across the counter.

I was just wondering how to get it out of the kitchen without being detected when a sudden movement caused me to look up. There, heading straight for me, was the cook. In his upraised hand was a giant cast-iron skillet.

For a horrible moment I just stood there, completely paralyzed. Finally, faced with the possibility of certain mutilation, if not death, I took the only way out. I dropped the steak and vaulted off the counter. The speed with which I raced out of the kitchen must have been a new world record.

There was no other thought in my mind except to get as far away as possible from my pursuer. I didn't even notice that the door I had gone through wasn't the one that led to the hallway. Without stopping, I headed blindly for the nearest shelter. Only sheer desperation enabled me to dive behind a partition and squeeze myself between two large boxes.

Exhausted, I slumped to the floor. My heart raced and my breath came in short gasps. Every muscle in my body ached from the sudden exertion. I closed my eyes while listening to the subdued snatches of conversation that intermingled with the clatter of silverware and china.

"Hey, Wes!"

The voice was close.

"Did you by any chance see a cat run through here?"

"A *what?*"

"A cat. Big and fat with black-and-white stripes

down his back. Looked almost like a skunk, actually."

"A cat who looks like a skunk?" The other man chuckled. "Oh, come on, Jake. You've got to be kidding."

"No, I'm not." The cook sounded annoyed. "There was a cat in the kitchen just a minute ago, swiping one of my steaks. When he saw me he dropped it and took off. I'm pretty sure he must have run out here."

Someone banged a glass down on the counter right over my head. "Well, if he did, I certainly didn't see him." As if by magic, a hand appeared right by my head, almost causing me to have a heart attack. It grabbed a bottle and vanished again. "And if any of the guests saw him, I would have heard about it by now."

My heart pounded. I wondered if I would live long enough to get back to the motel room. Why hadn't I stayed and watched "Perry Mason" with Josh and Winston? Then I wouldn't be in this terrible predicament now.

"Here, Jake." A glass slid across the counter. "Have a drink. It's on the house. You must have imagined the whole thing. Been working too hard, or something. Maybe you should take a few days off." There was the clinking of glass. "Nope, I can't remember ever having seen a cat loose around here. If people bring their pets, they're supposed to keep them locked up in their rooms. Never had any problem with that, as far as I know."

The cook finally left, still insisting that a cat had tried to steal his food. For my life I couldn't understand what he was griping about. I had left the steak there, hadn't I? And besides, they probably had plenty more in the freezer.

Already I felt better, although I still had no idea how I ever would get back to our room. By now I had managed to figure out that I had taken shelter right under a bar counter. The bartender was standing only a couple of feet away from my hiding place. All I could see, of course, were his jeans-clad legs and his boots.

Judging by the sounds—not to mention the smells, which made my stomach grumble—people were eating and drinking, if not in the bar itself, at least somewhere close by. I assumed the Carters were among the diners, which was comforting, although I wasn't exactly anxious to run into them.

For all I knew the bar would stay open all night. I might as well make a run for it now—and the sooner the better, too. If Mr. C. returned to the room before me and found that I was gone . . .

I decided that, first of all, I needed to find out

where the doors were. This was bound to be tricky, especially with the bartender at such close quarters. With a fervent prayer that he wouldn't suddenly look down, I eased myself quietly out from behind the boxes. Then, one step at a time, I moved toward the end of the bar.

Eventually I reached the point where I would be able to see the rest of the room. To make sure that the bartender's attention was on other things, I paused and looked over my shoulder. So far, all I had seen of him had been his legs from the knees down. Now, when my eyes took in the rest of him, I received the shock of my life.

The bartender, a mean-looking guy if ever I saw one, had exactly the same kind of slouch mustache as the bad guy in the John Wayne movie. Around his waist was an ammunition belt and hanging on his hips were two six-shooters.

Frozen into immobility by the sight of the guns, I continued to watch in horror as he removed one of them from its holster. After adjusting the grip he proceeded to raise it slowly and deliberately. It was obvious to me that he was aiming it at someone on the other side of the counter. Then his finger curled around the trigger. . . .

# ELEVEN

Transfixed, I stared at the gun while bracing myself for the sound of the shot.

Then, just as slowly, his finger uncurled and he put the gun back in its holster.

Weak from relief, I sank down to the floor. Wow! That had been close. But since when did motel employees carry weapons? And what kind of place was this, anyway?

After taking a few deep breaths to steady my nerves, I leaned forward and took a peek at the rest of the room. Standing at a table with her back to me was a girl dressed in a fringed Western shirt, blue jeans, and cowboy boots. She, too, had a pearl-handled revolver in a holster on her hip. A little farther away was another girl in a similar outfit, also armed. I felt the blood drain from my face. This was worse than I had imagined. It was obvious now that there was a whole gang of them.

A third girl was making her way between the tables, carrying a tray of food above her head. I had to admit that their idea to pretend to be just ordinary waitresses was pretty clever. Not that it had me fooled for a second, of course. If Josh and Winston could see this, they'd stop doubting. This was a saloon full of trouble.

I wondered how the gang had been able to take over the place so completely. But armed as they were, it had probably been easy. My guess was that the real staff was bound and gagged and locked up somewhere.

Now I spotted the Carters at a table over by the window. Apparently unaware of the dangerous situation, they were laughing and talking while finishing their desserts. Even B. C., who was sitting in a high chair, was smiling and waving his arms.

Seeing them like that, so carefree and happy, made me wish we were all home again, with me curled up in my favorite basket on the bookcase and the rest of the family busy with their everyday tasks.

Feeling very sorry for myself, I sniffled a couple of times. I didn't want to be stuck behind a bar all by myself, surrounded by desperadoes. The responsibility of protecting everybody all the time was just too much. I sniffled again. If only I could have Josh and Winston to help me.

Slowly I crawled back behind the counter. The task ahead seemed almost too monumental to be tackled. Not only would I have to come up with a way to warn the Carters so they could escape, I also had to avoid being caught myself. There was, of course, no way of keeping the outlaws from following us upstairs. Except, I thought miserably, for the fact that we probably wouldn't live long enough to get that far.

Cautiously, I peeked around the corner again. To my horror, one of the waitresses was now over by the Carters. Her left hand was on the back of B. C.'s chair while with her right hand she was twirling her gun around in the air.

Realizing that it was up to me to prevent a possible shoot-out, I hesitated no longer. Like a streak of lightning, I ran across the floor. Without even slowing down, I hurled myself up in the air and knocked the weapon out of her hand. The gun fell to the floor with a clatter. Dumbfounded, the waitress stared at me. Then she took off, screaming at the top of her lungs.

The Carters were glued to their chairs with faces frozen in expressions of stunned incredulity. B. C. had started crying. Desperate to get them to realize that they were still in mortal danger, I started clawing first at the tablecloth and then at Stevie's leg.

*"By God!"* Mr. C. abruptly sprang into action. "That does it." He threw his napkin down on the table and reached out to grab me. Relieved that someone finally was moving, I eluded his hands and headed for the door.

"I'll get him, Dad." Stevie attempted a tackle, which forced me to make a detour around another table.

"Wiggie-pooh!" Cilla wailed. "Come here, baby!" Good, I thought, she was coming, too. Now all I had to do was make them follow me upstairs.

"Well, I'll be damned! I guess Jake was right." I recognized the voice of the bartender, who suddenly was blocking my way. This made it necessary for me to take a shortcut between somebody's legs. The high-pitched scream that followed was rather unnerving. Some people, I thought, disgusted, didn't seem to have any idea how to behave in a restaurant.

I could hear the sounds of chairs being knocked over. One of the waitresses dropped her tray, splattering food all over the place. A blob of gravy landed on my nose. Gratefully, I licked it off.

By now I had completely lost my bearings. The only thing I was thankful for was that not one single shot had been fired. Maybe if I could keep everyone on their feet, trying to catch me, long enough . . .

Thank God, there was the door. I raced down the hallway past two startled guests. Up the stairs, around a corner, and straight down another hallway. Judging by the sounds behind me, the whole Carter family was close on my heels.

In vain I looked for the planter that I knew was only a few doors away from our room. Quickly, I turned another corner, hoping that this was it. Still no planter. Had I inadvertently reached the third floor instead of the second? It was possible.

Rounding yet another corner, I brought myself to a sudden halt. Panting and exhausted, I looked around. I knew at once that I had never been here before. In which direction should I go? The sound of voices was getting closer.

At that moment I happened to look at the wall above me. There, like an answer to my prayers, was an opening with a swing door, which was propped open by a bunch of scrunched-up towels. Without a moment's hesitation, I jumped up on the ledge and squeezed through the opening.

The interior was in total darkness. Instinctively I braced myself for when I would hit the floor, only for some reason there didn't seem to be a floor.

As I continued to fall down into the horrible black void, I knew that this was the end. Well, I thought bravely, at least I had given my life while saving the lives of others. My heroic death would, of course, make the headlines all over the world. Maybe the president would even declare a national holiday in my honor. And then there was the Nobel Peace Prize. . . .

My downward journey came to a sudden halt as I was engulfed by an unindentified substance that swallowed me up so completely that I was unable to breathe. Strangely enough, my last impression was that I was floating on a cloud. Then all went black.

# TWELVE

"**W**iggie, how *could* you?"

I examined my breakfast bowl with interest. Moist nuggets with bacon bits. Not bad. Bacon was one of my favorites.

"What on *earth* induced you to attack that poor waitress, scaring her half to death?" Cilla continued exasperatedly. "And then causing all that upheaval by running around the restaurant like a maniac?"

Enjoying my first mouthful, I wondered what the delay had been. Maybe Cilla had overslept. Personally, I had been awake since seven, listening to my grumbling stomach. Now it was almost eight o'-clock.

"Do you realize that Dad has to pay for the food that got ruined when the other waitress dropped her tray? Not to mention the broken china?"

For some reason I was famished this morning. This was probably because of all the exercise I'd had last night. I was sure I had lost at least a couple of pounds as a result. Maybe even more.

"Dad said that as soon as we get to Moscow he'll take you to the vet." She sighed. "He even suggested it might be a good idea for you to see a psychiatrist again."

At the mention of the vet I stopped chewing. Then when I heard the other bad word I almost choked on my food. A *shrink*? Again?

Last year Dr. Matson, the vet back home, had referred me to an animal psychiatrist. Not that I needed to see one, of course. It had just been another of Dr. Matson's sadistic attempts to get even with me. *He* was the one who needed to see a shrink, not me. How someone as mentally deranged as that man could be allowed to practice medicine was a mystery to me. Dangerous, that's what he was. Definitely dangerous. I hoped the vets out in Moscow would turn out to be different.

"I'm sorry you had to spend the night out in the

car, Wiggie-pooh, but as you can understand, the motel manager was extremely upset by your behavior. He even suggested that you might have rabies and that this was why you went crazy. Dad had to show him your vaccination certificate to prove that you had had all your shots."

*Rabies?* Well! I was so shocked that for a moment I almost lost my appetite. What a terrible thing to accuse a guest of, I thought indignantly. No wonder the motel was almost empty. And how come *he* didn't have to prove that he had had all his shots?

Now Cilla sighed again. "Well, you have to admit, Wiggie, that your behavior was peculiar, if not downright bizarre. You have no idea how embarrassing it was to have to tell the manager that you had jumped down the laundry chute." She shook her head at the memory. "And when we came down to the basement and looked in the cart that held all the laundry and you were lying there like a rag doll, well . . . that was scary. I really thought you were dead, you know. And you could have been. You could have broken your neck. The manager thought you were dead, too, because he said, 'Well, I guess you'll have to get yourself another cat.' Right then I could have pushed *him* down that chute." Cilla clamped a hand over her mouth and giggled. "Not that he would have fit into it, of course. Not with his stomach."

I licked up the last morsel of food. That had really hit the spot. Too bad there wasn't any more.

"Good thing Dad bought you this." Before I had a chance to protest she had snapped the leash onto my collar. "The manager said that if he saw you loose again," Cilla swallowed, "he'd call the humane society."

We walked around the lawn area behind the motel for a while. I squatted right under the window of the manager's office, but unfortunately Cilla dragged me away before I had time to do anything.

Pretty soon she put me back in the car. Then she went inside. Because of what had happened, the family was not having breakfast at the motel. I assumed they were all mad at the manager for treating me like a criminal. Really, I thought resentfully, I should go ahead and sue them. This was supposed to be a free country. Didn't they know that discrimination was illegal, not to mention unconstitutional?

The fact that I was a cat didn't give the manager the right to treat me the way he did. Besides, there was a large sign outside the office door that said *Pets Welcome.* But maybe he hadn't read it. Come to think of it, he probably couldn't even read.

"Is it true, old pal, that you staged a riot last night?" Winston asked when we were all settled in the car.

109

*"Riot?"* I raised my eyebrows. *"Riot?* Of course not. Where on earth did you hear that?"

Winston scratched his belly. "Stevie and Cilla were talking about it. Stevie said you practically wrecked the restaurant. Isn't that why you had to spend the night in the car?"

"Nonsense," I replied rather frostily. "On the contrary, it was thanks to me that there *wasn't* a riot. Or whatever you want to call it."

Gwendolyn asked timidly, "You mean that nothing happened at all?"

"Well." I rubbed my neck, which was itching from my collar. "Remember the movie we watched last night? The one with John Wayne? And you both said that those days were past?"

"Sure." Josh suppressed a yawn. "What about it?"

"You were wrong," I said earnestly. "Those days are not past. Last night"—I paused to change position. My right hip was still sore from my fall down the laundry chute—"last night, as I was taking my evening stroll, I happened to walk past the restaurant downstairs. And what do you suppose I saw?"

"People," Josh replied.

"Food."

"The Carters."

I shook my head. "I saw the bartender pull out a gun."

At last I had their undivided attention.

"A *gun?*"

"That's right."

Winston chuckled uncertainly. "Ha, ha, you're just kidding."

"I swear," I said.

"So what did he do with it?" Josh said interestedly. "Shoot you, ha, ha, ha?"

"Very funny," I said frostily. "Of course he didn't shoot me or I wouldn't be here now."

"You could be a ghost, ha, ha." Josh went into convulsions. "Except we can't see through you."

"Just ignore him," Winston said. "What did the bartender really do?"

"Nothing. He pointed it at someone, and after a minute or so, he put the gun back in the holster."

Josh sniffled and wiped his eyes. "Is that all?"

"No," I snapped irritably, "it isn't. Now, will you quit interrupting?"

Again I adjusted myself. Was it possible that my hip bone was fractured? Not that I was complaining, mind you. My pioneer heritage had always enabled me to endure pain and hardship that would bring others to their knees.

"At first," I said, "I thought I had imagined the whole thing. I mean, normally bartenders don't wave guns around at their customers, do they? But just in case there was something fishy going on, I moved inside the door so I could keep an eye on the table where Mrs. C. and the others were sitting. Fortunately, it was pretty dark in there, so the chances of my being seen were minimal."

"What were they having?" Gwendolyn asked.

I stared at her. "What was who having?"

"The Carters, of course. What were they eating?"

"What were they . . . For *heaven's sake,*" I said irritably, "how do I know? I wasn't watching their plates."

Josh said impatiently, "Never mind her. Go on, Wiggie."

"Well, there were several waitresses in the restaurant, carrying around trays with food and clearing tables. I must admit that I didn't pay much attention to them. I was too busy watching the bartender. Anyway, eventually one of the waitresses brought dessert for Mr. C. and the others. She . . ."

"I wonder if they all had the same thing?" Gwenny said pensively.

I took a deep breath and counted to five. "How do you expect me to know what they had?" I exploded. "I was over by the door."

"Well, there is no need to yell," she said. "I was just wondering, that's all. Usually parents order things like cheesecake or pie, while the kids . . ."

"For heaven's sake, let him finish his story."

"Thanks, Winston. Where was I again . . . ?"

"The waitress brought dessert. . . ."

"Oh yes." I cleared my throat. "Well, she put the plates down on the table. Then she kind of leaned against Mr. C.'s chair, and then . . ." I paused dramatically. ". . . then she, too, pulled out a gun."

Now Josh stared at me, mesmerized. "You're *kidding.*"

"No, I'm not. Before I knew it she started waving it around in front of Mr. C. She was saying something to him, but of course I was too far away to be able to hear. Quite possibly she was challenging him to a showdown at high noon.

"I tell you, for a second I was so shocked I couldn't move. I mean, one person with a gun was bad enough, but *two?*" I looked around at my pals. "Then, of course, I sprang into action. Without a moment's hesitation, I ran across the room and hurled myself at her. Just as she was about to aim the gun at me, I knocked it out of her hand."

"Wow!" I could hear Josh let out his breath. "And then what happened?"

I shrugged. "Well, since she no longer had a gun, she decided she might as well make a run for it. I had been expecting something like that, of course, so when she took off I went after her. Unfortunately, some of the guests had the same idea, while others were just trying to get out of the restaurant. Because of that, the situation was pretty confusing. One waitress dropped her tray, I know that. I myself lost track of the one I was chasing and, as far as I know, she managed to get away."

"Wow," Josh said again. "But what about the bartender? What happened to him?"

"I don't have the faintest idea. I imagine he realized the game was up and that he'd better save his own skin."

"But they were in on this together, weren't they?"

"I guess so. It would be too much of a coincidence to have two sets of outlaws plan a holdup at the same time in the same place."

For a while we were silent, contemplating all that had happened.

"But why did the waitress pick the Carters?" Winston said, puzzled. "I mean, Mr. C. doesn't have a lot of money. And"—he scratched his chest—"even if he did, the crooks wouldn't have known that. And you can't say that they *look* rich."

I thought about Stevie's frayed cut-offs and his sneakers, which were smelly and full of holes. "No," I agreed, "but then I don't think they were picked because of their money. I think it could as well have been any of the other guests. It's possible that she intended to keep the whole family at gunpoint while the the rest of them collected everybody's money. I guess we'll never really know."

Now Gwenny's eyes were full of horror. "You mean they were going to rob all the people in the restaurant? How awful!"

"Well," I said with a sigh, "as we know, they didn't succeed. It just goes to show, though, that the Wild West still is pretty wild."

"I wonder why all these exciting things always happen to you and never to me?" Josh complained.

I gave him a pitying smile. "The answer to that, my dear friend, is very simple. Instead of staying in my room to watch television, I go after adventure." I gave my chest a final lick. "My noble ancestors crossed the ocean in pursuit of freedom in a new world and they ended up as marshals' deputies out in the rugged West. Since I have their blood in my veins, I, too, venture out in search of action." My eyes took on a faraway look. "Who knows what my final destiny may be."

"Oh, Wiggie," Gwendolyn breathed. "You sound so . . . dashing. We're so lucky to have you around to protect us."

"I know," I said.

# THIRTEEN

*"T*hrough *the da-a-ark and grues-a-a-am fo-ore-est . . ."*

Josh held onto the long notes at least twice as long as necessary. To get away from the grating sound, I tried to bury my head in my blanket.

*"Where the wi-i-ild beasts ma-a-ake their ho-o-ome . . ."*

As usual, his voice cracked on the high notes. Pausing briefly to clear his throat, he continued undaunted.

*"Went the bra-a-ave and fearle-e-ess hunter . . ."*

"Josh, *please!*" I held my paws over my ears. "Is that the only song you know?"

"*I-i-in search of the gi-i-a-nt . . .*" He stopped abruptly. Then he started over. "*I-i-in search of the gi-i-a-nt . . .*" Again he stopped. His face had a puzzled expression. "*I-i-in search of the gi-i-a-nt . . .*" He tried for the third time. Now his voice held somewhat less enthusiasm.

"For heaven's sake," Winston exclaimed, ". . . a giant what? Can't you get it over with so we can have some peace and quiet?"

Josh still looked puzzled. "I don't remember," he said. "It rhymed with home. . . ." He scratched his head.

"Probably *gnome,*" I said tiredly.

"It's supposed to be an animal."

"How about *bear?*" Gwendolyn looked pale and drawn, but then we probably all did after almost an hour of listening to Josh's musical renderings.

"That doesn't rhyme with home."

"I know." She sighed. "But at least it's an animal."

Josh sank into deep concentration. From time to time he grunted, and once he burped rather noisily. Both were a great improvement over his singing.

Gradually, I began to doze off. Gwendolyn was already asleep. Winston's ears were twitching, a sure sign that he was dreaming.

*"I-i-in search of the gi-i-a-ant . . ."*

I came awake with a jerk. Gwendolyn sat up and rubbed her eyes, looking bewildered. Winston had jumped to his feet and was barking.

We all turned accusingly to Josh, who now sat with his mouth open, staring into space.

Slowly, he focused his eyes on us. "I almost had it, guys," he said. "It was right on the tip of my tongue. Let me try again. . . ."

The three of us crowded him into a corner. Winston said threateningly, "If we *ever* hear that song again . . ."

"What was Winston barking at?" Mrs. C. looked over her shoulder.

Cilla, who was slumped in the back seat, engrossed in a teen romance book, said absentmindedly, "I don't know." After a moment she put the book down. "I think they are all just getting tired of being cooped up in the car. Josh has been moaning and crying ever since we left McDonald's."

"Dona . . ." B. C. shouted enthusiastically. "Dona . . . dona . . ."

"Did you hear that, Mom? He's trying to say McDonald's. Isn't he smart?" Cilla gave B. C. a hug and a kiss. "Good boy."

Mrs. C. laughed. "I'm not so sure I want him to

start talking," she said. "When you were little, once you started you never stopped. It used to drive me up the wall." She laughed again, adding, "Why don't you give the cats some of those Chewy-chips or whatever they are called? And Winston can have the steak bone we got at the supermarket."

A few minutes later we were enjoying our unexpected snack. Even Josh seemed, at least for the moment, to have forgotten his musical activities.

After a while Winston said, "I must say that the scenery around here is pretty impressive."

I looked out the window. We were presently following a winding road that ran parallel with the river below. Dark-green forest covered the hillside, and somewhere in the distance ahead I could see the hazy outline of a mountain. I had to agree with Winston. Against the backdrop of a perfectly clear blue sky, it was indeed breathtaking.

"What state did you say this was?" Gwenny asked.

"Montana." We had passed a sign some hours ago that said, *Welcome to Montana. Drive carefully.* "Sure beats North Dakota. Why anyone would ever want to live there, I don't know."

"Me, neither," Gwenny agreed. "I've never seen anything so flat."

"I wonder what Idaho looks like." Josh looked up from the water bowl.

119

So far I hadn't given much thought as to what our new home state would be like. My focus had been on the trip and its hardships and dangers.

"It's probably mostly wilderness," I offered tentatively. "I assume that Moscow is the largest town in the state. At least, I've never heard of any other."

"What do you think our house will look like?" Gwenny wanted to know.

"Well." I shrugged. "First of all, *house* may not be the right word for it. Log cabin is probably a better definition." Not wanting to paint a too discouraging picture, I added hurriedly, "But I'm sure Mr. C. picked something pretty comfortable."

"I heard Mrs. C. mention once that it's not actually in town," Gwenny said thoughtfully. "I wonder how it will be, living in the country?"

I had to admit that this was the first I'd heard about it. Country, huh? I scratched my nose while wondering what kind of wild animals we would be surrounded by. Mountain lions, probably. And what about wolves . . . ?

"Just imagine." Winston stretched and yawned. "Only one more night and we'll be there."

"And," Gwenny said, "only one more day stuck in this car."

Winston grunted. "I know what you mean. Sometimes I have a feeling we've been on the road for weeks and weeks and weeks. . . ."

"That reminds me," Josh said suddenly. "Listen to this, guys." He cleared his throat. *"On the road, on the road, on the roo-a-ad to Id-a-a-ho-o-o . . ."*

"I'm sorry, Wiggie-pooh." Cilla stuck her head inside the car. "But it looks like you'll have to stay here tonight." She climbed in and shut the door. Then she picked me up and hugged me. "I tried to get Dad to let me bring you inside until bedtime, but he said no. Can't say I blame him, either. When I think of all the trouble you've gotten into since we left home . . ." Sighing deeply, she planted a kiss on my nose.

We sat in silence for a while. I snuggled up in the crook of her arm. What would I ever do without Cilla? No matter what happened, she was always on my side.

"I think I finally figured out why you attacked that waitress," she said after a moment. "You thought she was going to use the gun to hurt somebody, didn't you? You didn't know it was just a fake gun that was part of her uniform. So what you did, Wiggie-pooh, was very, very brave. If it had been a real gun, you could have gotten killed, too."

121

Gratefully, I rubbed my face against her shirt. At least she didn't think I had gone crazy.

"I tried to explain all this to Dad, but I don't think he listened to a single word. He just kept on saying over and over that you had finally flipped your lid."

*Well!* If that wasn't an outrage. . . . Whatever happened to family loyalty? Not that I was really surprised, of course. After all, Mr. C. had been perfectly happy to leave poor Gwendolyn behind at that supermarket parking lot. *He* had seen that Gwenny wasn't in the back of the car with Josh and me. But did he care? Of course not. What's one cat more or less? A few more days on the road and Mr. C. would probably lose B. C. or Stevie somewhere, too, and not even bat an eye.

Here I paused. Come to think of it, losing Stevie wouldn't be such a bad idea. Life would certainly be a lot more peaceful. I dwelled on this pleasant prospect for a moment. Fortunately for Stevie, I wasn't as unfeeling and careless as Mr. C. I, for one, would never let my personal preferences override my concern for the family. Even Stevie, I thought resignedly, belonged with the rest of us. Someday (like fifteen years from now), he might even turn into a normal human being.

"Well, Wiggie-pooh, I'd better go back in or Mom will wonder where I am. We are having dinner in our room tonight. There is a microwave oven in the lobby. I think we're having soup and sandwiches. Mom found a cake at half price, so we'll have that for dessert." Cilla returned me to my basket. "I'll come out later with your dinner. Maybe even some leftover soup and a piece of cake. How's that?"

Cilla was as good as her promise. In addition to all the other goodies, she had brought me not only one but two large pieces of cake. With only one day left before our arrival in Moscow, she had tried on her favorite jeans and discovered that she couldn't even zip them up. Panicky at the prospect of having to wear something else, she had skipped dinner entirely and brought me her dessert.

I was more than happy to help her out, of course. After all, I thought virtuously, sacrifice was my middle name. I patted my tummy while emitting a discreet burp. That second piece of cake had perhaps been a little too much for my digestive system, but . . . I'd rather put up with a little discomfort myself than to have Cilla jeopardize her figure.

After taking me for a little stroll on the leash, Cilla had gone in to bed. With nothing better to do, I now decided to pop off to sleep myself. Fortunately, the car was at the far end of the parking lot, away from the outside lights of the motel.

Rubbing my eyes, I made myself as comfortable

as I could. My tummyache would probably go away soon. Actually, I didn't mind in the least sleeping in the car. Out here all was quiet. No Stevie to worry about. No B. C. to wake up crying in the middle of the night.

When I opened my eyes again I had no idea what time it was. Nor did I at first know what had interrupted my sleep. It was still dark. Gradually, I became aware of a persistent rustling noise that probably was Cilla moving around in her sleep. Yawning, I was about to pass out again, when suddenly I remembered.

I was alone in the car. Presumably, the car was securely locked. But then—I felt a pang of apprehension—who was making all that noise?

Very carefully, I peeked over the edge of my basket. There, bending over something in the front seat, was the shadow of a man. The door on the passenger side was wide open. Evidently, he was going through our belongings, looking for things to steal.

No sooner had this fact registered in my brain than the thief suddenly vanished. A moment later the back door opened. Now his head and shoulders loomed alarmingly close as he began to unzip one of Cilla's bags. Instinctively, I pulled back, but even in the dark he must have noticed the movement.

For a second he remained absolutely still. I held my breath. Maybe he hadn't seen me. But then he reached for my throat. . . .

I just sat there as if hypnotized, watching the hands move steadily closer. Then, unexpectedly, the thief lunged forward.

# FOURTEEN

The sudden move finally prompted me into action. Instinctively, I jumped aside to avoid being caught. Then, with a loud cry, I slipped between his arms and threw myself at his face. The attack took him completely by surprise. When I dug my claws into his cheeks, there was a muffled scream. Furiously, I scratched at his face and hands while he made fruitless attempts to protect himself.

By now he was crouching on the floor of the back seat. Pretty soon I figured I had probably done enough damage to his face to put him out of action for the remainder of the night. With some difficulty, I untangled my claws from his hair and jumped up on the backrest of the driver's seat. The thief still continued to shield his face with his arms as he stumbled outside, kicking the door shut with his foot.

I spent a few moments catching my breath. Then I jumped out of the car through the front door, which the thief had left wide open. Although I wasn't able to see him, I could hear occasional muffled curses as he made his way across the yard in the dark.

Anxious not to lose track of him, I decided to take a shortcut through the shrubbery. I wanted to make sure he really was leaving. Not that I thought he would break into any more cars. No, I thought with satisfaction, not after the treatment I had given him.

I wondered if Mr. C. realized the danger he had exposed me to by forcing me to sleep in the car. If it hadn't been for my noble pioneer heritage and my fearless character, I would probably be dead now. As I envisioned myself being strangled by those big, ugly hands, I shivered. It had been a very close call.

Not that Mr. C. would care if I got killed, of course. No, I thought resentfully, he would probably be more upset by the fact that the car had been broken into than by finding my poor mutilated body inside it.

With these thoughts going through my mind, I squeezed my ample body through the bushes that separated the parking lot from the lawn area. I don't know what I expected to see when I came to the other side, but whatever it was, it wasn't this. . . .

There, right in my path, was a huge black bear.

The mouth had opened into a ferocious snarl that showed all his sharp teeth. The black, beady eyes glistened with fury and he had one front paw already lifted, ready to strike.

To be in mortal danger again so soon after just having escaped the jaws of death was simply too much. Why was I always the one to be caught in these perilous situations? Why not Josh or Winston? For that matter, why not Mr. C.? Why did it always have to be me?

Although I had, at the beginning of our trip, envisioned all kinds of dangers that might befall us, I must admit that at no time had I expected to have to contend single-handedly with a bear.

Overcome by a sudden wave of fury, I felt the blood rush through my veins at twice its normal speed. Without a thought to the possible consequences, I launched into my second enemy attack in less than ten minutes.

I used the same strategy as I had in my fight with the burglar. Hoping to keep those enormous paws from reducing me to pulp and the giant jaws from tearing me to shreds, I clawed and scratched frantically at his legs and chest.

I had no illusions of seriously injuring this wild beast. To someone that size my pitiful attempts were probably merely an irritation. No, my hope was to get him confused enough that I'd be able to make a safe getaway.

For what seemed an eternity I fought a desperate battle for my life, but all too soon I felt my strength diminish. Despite my outstanding physical condition, my previous adventure had obviously taken its toll. Now I began to have difficulty breathing, and my body was turning numb from exhaustion.

In a last supreme effort, I gathered my reserves of energy and dug my teeth into the bear's right leg. Despite the foul taste and his attempts to shake me off, I somehow managed to hang on. By sheer luck I must have hit a vital nerve of some kind, because all at once the bear stumbled and fell down on its side. A couple of tremors shook his body and then he was still.

The outcome was so unexpected that for a moment I remained immobile, still hanging onto his leg. Then I quickly abandoned the unconscious animal and once more squeezed myself through the bushes.

Completely at the end of my strength, I dragged myself into a comparatively safe spot between two rosebushes. Then I collapsed on the ground and closed my eyes.

# FIFTEEN

"**H**ey, guys!"

Even in my dazed condition I recognized Stevie's high-pitched voice.

"Hurry up! Come and see what happened to the bear!"

Doors slammed. More lights were turned on. They didn't reach as far as the shrubbery where I was lying, which was just as well. I was still stunned by my sudden victory over the bear. Not that I had ever had any doubts about the outcome, of course.

132

After all, courage was my middle name. Like my pioneer ancestors, I had simply refused to run away when faced with danger.

Although my whole body ached, I didn't think anything was broken. Even so, I decided right now I'd rather not be seen by anyone.

Soon there were dozens of people out in the yard, clustered around the bear, which was lying on its side.

"Somebody tried to tear him to pieces."

"Did you see this leg?"

"Look, there are tufts of fur everywhere."

I hoped they realized that although I had rendered the bear unconscious, it was bound to wake up again. This time they'd better not count on me. One bear fight was enough to last me a lifetime.

The motel guests, most of them in robes and pajamas, were animatedly discussing what had happened.

"Who would attack him in the first place?" someone wanted to know.

"A dog probably."

"Must have been more than just one."

"What about coyotes?"

"No way. Not this time of year."

"Why not?"

"Take my word for it. I know."

"You mean there aren't any coyotes around here?"

The two started arguing. Another man said, "You didn't let Fluffy out, did you, Sally?"

"*Fluffy?* You think I'd let *Fluffy* outside in the middle of the night? Are you crazy or something?"

"Just wanted to make sure, honey, that's all."

"Well, don't you go accusing my baby. . . . Besides, since when does a poodle go after a bear?"

Then I heard Mrs. C. "Well," she said in a tone of relief, "at least it wasn't Winston. He's still asleep."

Stevie made one of his weird noises. "The only one who'd be dumb enough to attack a bear," he said gleefully, "would be fat, stupid Wiggie. Ha, ha."

I suppressed the urge to knock him down with one of my flying tackles. Maybe, I thought, I could feed him to the bear as a late-night snack.

At long last the motel manager arrived. Evidently he didn't like the idea of having all his guests wandering around in the middle of the night because he began to herd them back inside. No, he assured them, there was nothing to worry about. Everything was under control. They could all go back to bed.

"Mom," Cilla said plaintively, "don't you think we should check on Wiggie? He must be frantic, listening to all this commotion while being locked up in the car."

Without waiting for Mrs. C.'s reply, I scrambled to my feet. Ignoring my sore muscles, I headed for the parking lot, taking the shortcut through the bushes.

I had almost reached the car when I heard a familiar voice behind me.

"Wiggie?"

I stopped and turned around. "Josh? Is that you? What are you doing here?"

"Cilla left the window open. But how come you're not in the car? Who let you out?"

"Well . . ." I began. Then I suddenly became speechless as I remembered the thief. What had happened to him? It was strange how my encounter with the bear had made me forget everything else.

"Well, what?" Josh said impatiently.

"Well . . ." I took a deep breath and launched into my story. "You probably won't believe this, old pal, but there was this guy who broke into our car and tried to steal something, only I jumped him and scratched his face, so he took off, and then I was attacked by this enormous black . . ."

"Wiggie-pooh!" Unexpectedly, I found myself whisked up into Cilla's arms. "My poor baby!" She squeezed my battered body until I almost passed out.

"And Josh is here, too." Mrs. C., clutching her robe, sounded bewildered.

"Poor Wiggie," Cilla cooed. "What happened? Who let you out of . . ." She stopped short as she caught sight of the car. The front door was still wide open. Various items had spilled out of a duffel bag, which lay on the ground. "Mom!" she exclaimed in dismay. "Look at this."

"Oh, no . . ." Mrs. C. hurried over to the car. After a look at the mess inside, she said, "Are you sure you locked the doors again when you brought Wiggie his food?"

"Mom, I know I did." Cilla was almost in tears. "I swear."

"Wiggie!" Josh's voice sounded strangled. Through the corner of my eye I saw that Mrs. C. now was holding him by the scruff. "You mean somebody really did break into the car?"

"Of course," I said irritably. I wiggled my body in a futile attempt to get out of Cilla's overprotective arms. "I told you. He was just going through the stuff in the front seat when I woke up."

"Wow! I bet that scared you to death."

I eyed him coldly. "Certainly not," I said. "I simply spent a few moments assessing the situation.

136

Then I took aim and hurled myself straight at his face." I recalled with satisfaction how startled the thief had been. "I kept on clawing at him until he dropped everything and ran for his life."

Josh looked impressed. "Lucky thing he didn't stay around to beat you to a pulp. Ha, ha. You must have been relieved to see him disappear."

There were times when Josh's behavior was definitely juvenile. "On the contrary," I countered frostily, "as a law-abiding citizen, I realized that it was my civic duty to capture the thief before he had a chance to continue his criminal activities."

Josh stared at me. "You mean you went after him?"

"Naturally."

"So, where is he?"

"Well," I said with an attempt at modesty, "doubtlessly, I would have caught him had I not been attacked by this giant, vicious . . ."

Once again I was interrupted, this time by Mrs. C., who already had handed Josh over to Stevie. Now she was telling him to bring both of us inside.

"But I want to watch the police," Stevie protested.

His father, who had suddenly appeared, and who evidently was not in the best of moods, said sternly, "Do as you are told. Besides, the police aren't even here yet."

137

Muttering to himself, Stevie left, dragging his feet. Josh and I were nearly choked to death by his careless grip around our necks. As soon as he got inside the room, he unceremoniously dumped us on the floor. We lay there gasping for air for several minutes.

"Too bad," Josh muttered vindictively, "that the bear out there isn't alive, or I'd have him chase Stevie around for a while."

Had I heard right? "Are you by any chance referring to the bear in the yard?" I asked.

Josh yawned. "I guess so. Unless, of course, there is another one around." Stifling another yawn, he climbed up on the bed, where he proceeded to make himself comfortable.

My heart skipped a beat. Could it really be true? Had I inadvertently killed the bear? It seemed incredible, but perhaps I had underestimated my own strength.

"Uh . . . did it . . ." I wondered how to phrase my question. "I mean . . . eh . . . was the bear badly . . . uh . . . injured?"

"Didn't you see him?" Josh sounded surprised. "You must have been the only one. Well, from what I could tell, some of the fur on his face had been ripped off. He also had a big hole in one leg where the stuffing was coming out. Then somebody said . . ."

"*Stuffing?*"

"You know, whatever is inside him. It looked like sawdust but it could have been something else. After all, it was pretty dark out there."

"*Stuffing?*" I repeated. What was he talking about?

Josh frowned. "Something the matter, Wiggie? You're acting kind of funny."

*Stuffing?*

"No," I mumbled. "I'm fine."

"I guess when you really think about it, it's kind of strange to have a stuffed bear in the yard," Josh went on. "A real one, I mean. The manager told Mr. C. how he bought it five years ago from somebody who was a taxi . . . uh . . . taxi something. . . ."

"Taxidermist," I said automatically.

"That's it. Then Mr. C. said, 'It sure looks real,' and the manager said, 'It sure does,' and that's why he always tells his guests about it as soon as they arrive, so they won't get scared thinking it's alive."

The bear was *stuffed?* It couldn't be.

"Wiggie?" Josh looked worried. "Are you listening? Your eyes look glassy. Are you sure you're all right?"

139

*Stuffed?* That meant I hadn't killed the bear. Not even knocked it unconscious.

"Wiggie!"

With an effort I focused my attention on him. "Uh . . . did you say something?"

"I asked what the reason was for you not catching up with the thief?"

"Thief?" I looked at him blankly. "Oh . . . you mean the *thief*! Well." I scratched my head. "He . . . er . . . ran off. Then I guess he must have knocked over the bear because I . . . uh, I . . . tripped over it. When I got back on my feet the guy was gone, of course, and pretty soon the lights went on and people started coming out, and . . . you know . . ."

Josh yawned again. "Well," he said sleepily, "at least you tried. Good night, old pal."

"Good night."

After some thought, I crawled way underneath the bed. It was a tight fit between the box spring and the floor, but I was prepared to put up with the discomfort. Good thing I wasn't the complaining type, but then, of course, I come from hardy pioneer stock.

I didn't really expect Mr. C. to try to put me back in the car for the rest of the night, but then you never knew. I'd rather not take any chances.

# SIXTEEN

The next morning I found to my surprise that, instead of being uncomfortably wedged in underneath the bed, I was comfortably curled up in a chair. I figured I must have slept pretty soundly not to have noticed when I was being moved. Gwendolyn and Josh had almost finished their breakfast. Mine was waiting, and I wasted no time digging in. After last night's strenuous exercise, I needed something to get my strength back.

After swallowing my first mouthful, I asked, "Where is everybody?"

"Everybody"—Josh licked the bottom of his milk bowl—"is at the manager's office talking to the police."

"The police are still here?" I thought they would have left a long time ago.

"They just came back," Gwenny informed me. "It looks like they have found the man who broke into the car."

"Well!" That was good news.

I hoped the police realized that without my intervention the thief wouldn't have been captured at all. If the crime had not been discovered until this morning, the thief could already have been hundreds of miles away. I was just about to point this important fact out to the others when the door opened and Cilla came in.

"Oh, there you are, Wiggie-baby." She reached down and picked me up. "You can finish your breakfast later. Right now the police want you."

Before I knew what was happening I was whisked out the door, which, a moment later, slammed shut behind us. I had a brief glimpse of Josh and Gwendolyn as they stared after me with open mouths. Curiosity was written all over their faces.

A few minutes later I was in a police car with Cilla and Mr. C. Two officers were up front. I found it rather alarming that no one said anything during the short ride. What was it all about, anyway? Why did the police want me? And where were we going?

It was comforting to feel Cilla's arms around me. Instinctively, I buried my face in her sweater. What if, I thought worriedly, they decided to prosecute because I had torn up the bear? What if they put me in jail? Would the Carters go on to Moscow without me?

I didn't look up until the car came to a halt outside the police station. Then I tried to make myself as small as possible. What would happen now?

"Remember," the younger of the officers cautioned us before we went inside, "Walker doesn't know you're coming. The scratches on his face and hands are pretty nasty. If he saw Wiggie at all before he was attacked, we should get some kind of reaction out of him now. His story is that he fell in the gravel in the driveway when he was drunk, which is ridiculous." The officer shook his head. "We had a doctor examine the scratches and there is no doubt that they were caused by an animal."

So that was why they had brought me here! I breathed a sigh of relief. I should have known better than to worry. Feeling distinctly better, I assumed a more dignified position on Cilla's arm. After all, it looked like the police wouldn't be able to prove their case without my assistance. It was lucky for

143

them that I had been born with nerves of steel. Fearlessly, without any thought of the extreme danger involved, I had risked my life in order to protect the lives and property of others.

The officer showed us into an empty room and told us to wait. Mr. C. walked back and forth. Cilla kept on rubbing my ears.

"Why is it taking so long?" she asked nervously.

"They are getting him from the jail, I guess."

A moment later the door opened and there he was, flanked by two guards. I recognized his black-and-red-checked shirt. I knew I would never have known him by his face, but then again, probably his own mother wouldn't have either, right now. He had at least a dozen ugly red streaks criss-crossing his face. One of his eyes was swollen almost shut, and he had bruises all over and bandages on both hands.

Unconsciously, I puckered up my face into a scowl. Then I waved my paws in the air and hissed. The moment the thief laid eyes on me he pulled back in alarm, crying, "Take him away. Don't let him get me again. Take him away. . . ."

As they say, the rest is history.

The chief of police personally went across the

144

street and bought two jumbo burgers and a large slice of cheesecake with whipped cream. I ate the whole thing while sitting on his desk.

"Darnedest cat I ever saw," he said, for the third time. "Fights like a devil and eats like a horse." After a moment he added, "And looks like a skunk."

I decided to overlook that last remark, since some of my more distinctive markings do indeed have certain similarities with those of that particular animal.

At that moment, the dispatcher came in and handed the chief a paper. He glanced at it for a few moments. Then he chuckled to himself.

"Looks like Walker is wanted by the police in three other states, too. For robbery, arson, breaking and entering, forgery, fraud, and a few other things. He is also known to carry a gun." The chief scratched his chin. "I guess Wiggie was lucky he didn't have one this time. Right, fella?" He poked a finger at my side.

At the mention of the gun I almost choked on my food. I didn't appreciate the poke either, but recognized the chief's underlying concern for my welfare.

"I reckon he wouldn't have had a chance to get the

145

gun out, anyway," remarked one of the other police-men.

The chief studied me for a moment. Then he said, "I reckon you're right, at that."

When we came back to the motel, Mrs. C. and Stevie were already waiting outside with their bags. We left shortly afterward. By the time I had filled my pals in on the latest developments, we had already crossed the border into Idaho.

"Oh, Wiggie," Gwenny said breathlessly, when I had finished, "you could have been killed."

Josh said, "You mean he actually had a gun?"

I gave my paw an unnecessary lick. "I guess I shouldn't even have mentioned it," I murmured. "It wouldn't have made the slightest difference to me, anyway, had I known. I only did what anyone else in my position would have done." Not that I really believed that anyone else would have been as brave as I, but the way I said it, it sounded good.

Once again I looked down at the medal that was hanging from a ribbon around my neck. It was actually an 1880 silver dollar with a bullet hole through it. The chief had taken it out of his wallet and Linda, the dispatcher, had contributed the ribbon.

"Got that dollar from my great-uncle," the chief

had said. "He made the hole while he was target shooting." Then he hung it around my neck. "Don't have any official medals for catching criminals, so I guess this will have to do. Sort of a reminder."

"And that bullet hole was really made by Jesse James?" Winston said now, staring at the medal. "How did the chief get it, then?"

"It originally belonged to his great-uncle."

"You mean he knew Jesse James?"

"The chief didn't say." I shrugged. "Probably didn't want to admit to having a relative who was an outlaw."

"The Wild West." Winston sounded wistful. "It must really have been exciting back then."

"Seems to me it's still pretty wild and exciting," I said dryly. "Too exciting for my taste."

Gwenny said dreamily, "I wonder what Moscow will be like?"

"I guess we'll soon find out. We'll be there this evening."

There was a brief silence. We looked at the trees flashing by.

Suddenly Josh said, "I heard Mr. C. mention that there are cougars around there."

"And bears," Gwenny added.

Bears? I decided it was time to change the subject. "How about some shut-eye?" I suggested. "I don't know about you guys, but personally I didn't get much sleep last night."

"Good idea," Winston rumbled.

"Fine with me." Gwenny yawned discreetly.

"How about it Josh, old pal?"

Josh winked at me.

"Yep," he said.

# About the author
# and illustrator

Born and raised in Sweden, author Elisabet McHugh
has traveled extensively throughout the world. She lived
in West Berlin and Australia before coming to the
United States, where she has lived since 1971. She is the
single parent of six adopted children and occupies a
large rambling house on ten acres in northern Idaho.
Her other books include *Raising a Mother Isn't Easy,*
*Karen's Sister, Karen and Vicki,* and *Beethoven's Cat,*
which was published by Atheneum in 1988.

Anita Riggio currently resides in Wethersfield, Connecti-
cut, and is an art instructor at the Hartford Art School
of the University of Hartford. Her picture book *Wake*
*Up, William!* was published by Atheneum in 1987. She
also illustrated Elisabet McHugh's previous book for
Atheneum, *Beethoven's Cat.*